"Sarah L. Johnson is an absolutely stunning talent. Her words strike true, and her stories are dripping with the very stuff that makes us Human."

~ Axel Howerton, Arthur Ellis Award-nominated author of *Hot Sinatra*, and *Furr*

"Johnson's stories often arouse and frighten in equal measure. A strong female voice has well and truly arrived in the dark fiction genre. Take her hand as she walks you through these eleven tales, but pray she doesn't let go."

~ Beavisthebookhead Blog

"Dark and honest, hauntingly beautiful and sharp, Ms. Johnson's prose will tear at you. Keep an eye on this lady, I think she will prove herself a force to be reckoned with in literature."

~ C.W. LaSart, Author of *Ad Nauseam*

Suicide Stitch
Eleven Stories

~

Sarah L. Johnson

EMP Publishing
Salem, Oregon
www.emppublishing.com

Suicide Stitch
Eleven Stories

ISBN: 978-0-6926613-2-1

Grateful acknowledgment is made by the author to the editors of the following publications, where many of these stories first appeared. All publication rights have reverted to the author.

"The First Wife" appeared in *Orthogonal Magazine*, January 2016 copyright © 2016 by Sarah L. Johnson.
"Five-Day Forecast" appeared in *Room Magazine*, January 2014 copyright © 2014 by Sarah L. Johnson.
"Heart Beating Still" appeared in *Erotica Apocrypha*, Freaky Fountain Press, September 2011 copyright © 2011 by Sarah L. Johnson.

Cover Design by Krisztian © Jennifer Word by Licensing Agreement c/o 99designs.com

ISBN: 0692661328 (paperback)
ISBN-13: 978-0-6926613-2-1 (paperback)

Printed in the United States of America

Contents

Thank You For Playing ~ ~ ~ ~ ~ ~ ~ 9

I Am Lost ~ ~ ~ ~ ~ ~ ~ 22

The First Wife ~ ~ ~ ~ ~ ~ 35

Five-Day Forecast ~ ~ ~ ~ ~ ~ 39

Heart Beating Still ~ ~ ~ ~ ~ ~ 52

Why(Y) ~ ~ ~ ~ ~ ~ 78

Three Minutes ~ ~ ~ ~ ~ ~ 81

Little Sister, Little Brother ~ ~ ~ ~ ~ ~ 93

A Ballad For Wheezy Barnes ~ ~ ~ ~ ~ ~ 140

Bridge ~ ~ ~ ~ ~ ~ 157

Suicide Stitch ~ ~ ~ ~ ~ ~ 172

Acknowledgments ~ ~ ~ ~ ~ ~ 186

About the Author ~ ~ ~ ~ ~ ~ 187

For my sister, without whom I wouldn't know how to tell a story, or use a semicolon.

~

Suicide Stitch

Eleven Stories

~

Thank You For Playing

~

Welcome to the neighborhood. It's the oldest community in Calgary and I've lived here a while. Perhaps you've passed my house once or twice, cutting through Inglewood and Ramsay on your way into Stampede Park. Maybe you've seen me strolling by in the morning while you sit on the patio at Gravity, drinking espresso and reading the paper. Or it could have been you that I saw, staggering out of the Ironwood at midnight and wandering with your friends down the sidewalk in search of a taxi. You see a lot of pedestrians in this area. And why not? These old streets have stories.

Walk with me, and I'll tell you mine.

~

The crossing signal chirped on the corner of 9th Avenue and 8th Street, where I stood in the rain in front of the barred windows of Fair's Fair Used Books. My good shoes splashed through puddles as I crossed the road, so lost in my thoughts that I narrowly missed being clipped by a police cruiser of all things. Based on how my latest job interview played out, it might have been better to let it paste me.

I shivered in my thin jacket as I headed down into Inglewood. Inside my hood, the rain sounded like a hail of thumbtacks falling from the sky. I just wanted to get home, fire up the computer and lose myself in the World of

Warcraft. But first, I'd go to Spolumbo's. I needed something glorious to wash away the bitter taste of rejection and old coffee. I needed purpose. I needed a sandwich.

What a morning. Five seconds after the introductory handshake, I knew the whole interview was a sham and they'd already decided to hire the manager's step nephew-in-law or whatever. Afterward, I plodded down the endless procession of Car2Go's lining the street like hardboiled eggs, and reached my Jetta just as it was being towed away. Watching my VW slide out of view, I felt the first drops splat on my head. Guess where I left my umbrella?

I'd been walking in the rain ever since.

I scuttled past the sandstone bricks of the Alexandra Centre, stopping when I saw the note. A yellow sticky note pasted to the black steel pole at the entrance to the dance hall. I leaned in for a closer look and read a single word in water-blotched ink.

LINCOLN

Coincidence, right? Thing is, I don't have the kind of name you find on a souvenir key chain. It's a dead American president, or a wealthy dad car. Not many guys in their thirties with that name. So why would someone write it on a sticky note and slap it on this pole outside the Alex? What were the odds that I would find it? I grabbed the soggy yellow square, stuffed it in my pocket, and kept walking.

~

Two days later, the rain turned into one of those heavy spring blizzards that slop two feet of snow overnight and bring the city to a standstill. But I couldn't stand still. I was out of coffee. So I booted up and shoveled my way out of my home – a bungalow hardly bigger than a doghouse, but corralled on all sides by an eight-foot fence. Inherited from my impressively paranoid grandmother. I had to walk to the Corner Store because I couldn't afford to bail out the Jetta. A few parking tickets piled on top of the impound fees added up to a tidy mountain of cash I couldn't spare in my jobless state. The snow wasn't helping in that regard. An interview I had lined up for that morning got cancelled.

I hiked up MacDonald Avenue, past Pop's Dairy Bar, to the corner of 8th where I saw a swatch of yellow stuck to the side of a brick house even smaller than mine. Another sticky note. I trudged through the snow and read the words, written in blue ballpoint.

Mrs. Chen is elderly and has arthritis.
Be a good neighbor and clear her walk.

I didn't do it because the note told me to. That's what I told myself anyway. I did it because the shovel was right there, propped against the porch, and I hated to think of an elderly woman trapped in her home, or worse, attempting to shovel a million pounds of wet spring snow herself. So I cleared her front walk, the sidewalk, and the walks of her neighbors, in case they were old and arthritic as well.

Sweating and exhausted, I replaced the shovel only to find a tiny Asian woman blinking at me through the screen of her front window. A person I'd never met, though we'd probably been neighbors for years.

"I heard a racket," she said.

"Um, hi," I said, panting. "I just...saw the shovel and...I hope you don't mind."

"That was thoughtful of you."

My thoughts had nothing to do with it, and I felt ashamed. I pointed toward MacDonald Avenue. "I live just down the hill, near the ice cream place. I'm Linc. Lincoln, actually, but my friends call me Linc."

She neither smiled nor frowned. Her eyes revealed only the nervous reflection of a sweaty man on her stoop who might be a serial killer for all she knew. Finally she nodded. "I'm Sally. My friends call me Mrs. Chen."

I started to laugh before I realized she wasn't kidding. Unbidden, an image of Chen Stormstout came to mind. Fighting panda, brewmaster, and binge drinker, from the lost continent of Pandaria.

Is that racist? For sure it's nerdy. I'm a nerdy racist.

I cleared my throat. "It's nice to meet you, Mrs. Chen. You have a good day."

Her eyes followed me down the sidewalk until I turned the corner. I pulled the note off the side of her house and tucked it into my pocket.

~

By the end of the week the snow was gone, and the poplars were loaded down with fat catkins, ready to release their cotton in another kind of annual blizzard. The cloudless afternoon beckoned through my front window and I decided to take a break from the job search and leveling up my night elf. A walk sounded good. Since my car got impounded, I'd been taking the ol' heel-toe express a lot.

Surprisingly, I didn't miss having wheels. I noticed things while walking that simply whizzed by in a blur while driving. The name of a street stamped into a sidewalk. The odd popularity of lime green front doors. A tree full of birdhouses, dozens of them, in all shapes and sizes. It wasn't too far from that tree that I found my next note. Stuck to the rusted steel shade of an old-fashioned lamp shining on the flashing yellow at the intersection of 19th Avenue and 8th Street. It took a bit of climbing, and I probably looked ridiculous, but I managed to snatch it down.

It's a beautiful day in our neighborhood, but not all neighbors are as fortunate as you. Stop into Red's Diner and order a fried egg sandwich to go. Take it down to the Bow River pathway. Someone under the 12th Street bridge is sure to appreciate a hot lunch.

I crumpled the paper and stuffed it into my pocket. Who'd left these notes? Were the quests meant for me, or were they plastered all over the neighborhood, waiting for any random pedestrian to find them? Was it part of some 'mind blowing' social experiment bound for viral Internet fame? Was there a bearded hipster with an iPhone hidden in a bush nearby? I thought about ignoring the note and going about my business, but what business? I had nothing else to do.

With a takeout container warming my hands, I headed across 9th Avenue to the river walk running behind Inglewood. I ambled along the path, listening to the icy rush of the Bow, running fast and deep with the spring melt. Clumps of grass still clung to the trees lining the riverbank, residual evidence of the flood two years ago.

Under the bridge I spotted a shaggy man in an army jacket hunkered down on some rocks, cigarette dangling from his lip as he stared at the river. Muradin Bronzebeard, valiant soldier and lost heir to the dwarven throne, wandering the kingdom with no memory of who he once was... *Okay, what is wrong with you? This is a real person, not some character in a stupid fantasy game.*

"Hi," I said, not knowing what else to say while standing in the middle of the path holding a takeout box.

The man raised a hand in tentative greeting. As I approached, he scrambled to his feet. "Not bothering no one," he said. "Got just as much right to be here as you."

The patched elbows of his army jacket were worn away, allowing the waffle weave of a grey thermal shirt to peek through. He'd burned holes in his gloves. Probably from his cigarettes. I thought of the recent snowstorm I'd weathered in my warm, dry house, angry over my cancelled job interview.

"Sorry," I said. "I didn't mean to disturb you, I just thought…" I reminded myself that it hadn't been my thought at all. Sure I knew homeless people existed, but did I ever think about them, really? I offered the box again. "Fried egg sandwich. Still warm."

"No kiddin'?" He accepted the box, pressed his nose to the lid and inhaled before opening it. "Over easy. This is my favorite. What are the odds?"

"Couldn't tell you," I said, casually glancing around. "Uh, this is going to sound weird, but did someone tell you I was coming?"

Bronzebeard transferred a partially chewed bite of sandwich into his cheek and gave me a wary side eye. "Someone tell you I'd be here?"

I shook my head. "How's the sandwich?"

"Just grand, and I sure do appreciate it. I'm Freddy. Short for Manfred."

"Linc. Short for Lincoln."

Bronzebeard, aka Freddy, guffawed. "Mother got it in her head that Manfred was dignified and such. But you, that's a Dad name if ever I heard one."

I surprised myself by laughing. "You're not wrong."

The conversation came to a slightly awkward end and I left him to finish his lunch. The sandwich smelled delicious. I figured next time I might come down with two takeout boxes.

~

Two weeks. No notes. I thought it was over. Not much had changed otherwise. Unemployed, with an incarcerated vehicle, and out of coffee. In the Corner Store, I ran into Chen Stormstout, crouched in the dairy aisle, rummaging through milk jugs in search of an expiry date set in the far-flung future.

"Morning, Mrs. Chen. Need any help?"

"Not unless you can find a jug of milk that'll stay fresh until I'm dead."

I grabbed the nearest carton of half and half without bothering to check the expiry. Mrs. Chen dropped a jug of two percent in her basket and used her glittery blue cane to hoist herself up. "I never buy green bananas, but for some reason milk needs to last forever. One day you too will be old and eccentric, Linc."

"Looking forward to it."

I followed her into the cereal aisle and grabbed a can of Maxwell house. Mrs. Chen selected generic bran flakes and Cap'n Crunch. Mrs. Chen was officially terrific. We paid for our meager groceries and stepped out into the overcast morning.

Mrs. Chen pointed east down 19th Avenue. "My friend, Gail, lives this way. She invited me for tea. I think she's overfeeding her cats again."

"Can I walk you?" I asked.

She grinned and gave me a shockingly hard whack with her blue warrior's staff. "Mashing on an old woman, are you?"

"Nothing but dishonorable intentions," I said, resisting the urge to rub my throbbing kneecap.

She handed me her grocery bag and the rubber foot of her cane tapped the sidewalk in an even cadence as we walked. In my periphery, I spotted a square of yellow stuck to a lamppost.

Did I stop to read that note? Did I even look at it closely as I walked by? No, I did not. I was hanging out with my neighbor and not in the mood to play dancing monkey.

"I'm glad winter is over," said Mrs. Chen. "The ice makes it so hard for me to get around."

"Totally," I agreed. "I didn't realize how brutal it could be until I lost my car."

Mrs. Chen grunted. "I've heard of people losing their keys, but it's a rare talent to lose a whole car."

"Yeah, well." I stuffed my hands in my pockets, where my fingers brushed against a crumpled piece of paper. "Mrs. Chen, you've lived in the area a long time, right?"

"Over fifty years."

"You know anything about these?" I uncrumpled the note in my pocket, the one with my name on it, and showed it to her. "Ever seen something like this before?"

She pushed my hand away and the *thump thump thump* of her cane accelerated. "This is an old neighborhood, Linc. Live here long enough, you'll see a lot."

"Someone's been leaving these for me."

She sighed and clutched the sleeve of my jacket. "What's the harm in playing along?"

After Mrs. Chen introduced me to Gail and her three monstrously obese felines, I took the long loop home. I thought hard about my situation as I trekked up 11th Street, past the muffler place and the feed co-op. If not for the notes, I'd never have met the unpredictable Mrs. Chen, and I wouldn't be having lunch a couple times a week with Freddy Bronzebeard. In Warcraft, I preferred to spend my time on quests, interacting with non-playable characters, but in Real Life there was something to be said for feeling connected to people.

~Thank You For Playing~

I felt good about how my life had changed since my car got dragged away to parking ticket prison. It wasn't just the exercise. Each step brought me closer to being a better version of myself, and I had the notes to thank for it.

I arrived home to find my front gate open, a headless magpie decorating my porch, and another note. A sticky note, not merely stuck, but tacked into my front door with a nail.

A picture worth more than a few words.

~

I'd been drawn into some kind of game, and Mrs. Chen's cryptic comment had me convinced I was only the latest in a long line of players. Awfully stupid of me, putting that first note into my pocket, a note that literally had my name on it. What was I supposed to do now? Call the cops? *Yes, officer. I'm being stalked by sticky notes challenging me to perform small acts of kindness...* No. The wise Chen Stormstout was right. Old neighborhoods have their secrets, and I felt weirdly protective of that. There seemed to be little harm in playing along. Refusing, on the other hand...well, there I wasn't so sure.

Three days after the frowny face, after I scooped up the dead bird and patched the sad little hole in my door, I found the next note. In truth, I'd spent the better part of the day looking for it. On 11th street, just before the road dips under the train tracks, there's a shrubby slope leading up to the Art Point Gallery. On the NO PARKING sign, a yellow square fluttered in the gusting wind. I climbed up and grabbed the note.

This area doesn't get much foot traffic, but it's still a part of our community and the wind blows in a fair amount of trash. Why not pitch in and pick up?

I found some black bin liners and a pair of work gloves anchored under a rock at the base of the sign. A train began its long rumble over the tracks above. I dropped the note in my pocket and donned the gloves. Then I shook open the trash bag and started gathering up fast food wrappers, Starbucks cups, and shivering strips of cellophane from cigarette packs.

~

Over the next couple weeks, I hardly played Warcraft at all. I had no time. I'd picked up so much garbage in so many places, I was sure people thought I was a convict performing community service. My daily quests took me to playgrounds, roadsides, and vacant lots, armed with nothing but gloves and a trash bag. How many experience points did picking up litter earn?

For expediency, or so I assumed, the notes began to appear on my front gate in the mornings. I never saw who left them. To be honest, I was afraid to look. If strike one was a dead bird, I didn't want to wind up with a boiled bunny rabbit, or a horse head on my pillow.

One sun-splashed morning, in late May, I found my front gate conspicuously noteless. I had an interview in the afternoon, and nothing but time to kill until then. Seemed like a good opportunity to swing by Gravity for lattés and power cookies before heading down to the river. Those cookies were magical, even with the walnuts, which I enthusiastically loathed and even went so far as to claim I was allergic to, in my desire to avoid them. Funny how you

18

could find yourself in love with something, even if one of the ingredients typically offended you to the core. Freddy Bronzebeard could take or leave the latté, but we were of like mind on the unique worth of the power cookie.

I took the long way around, as was my recent habit, along 11th Street and turning onto 10th Avenue, where I caught a glimpse of my reflection as I strolled past the glass front of Festival Hall. I stopped, hardly recognizing myself. My hair wanted cutting and I'd cultivated more than a bit of chin scruff. I'd also lost my vitamin D deficient pallor and the sedentary roll around my middle. I looked different. Healthy. Happy.

~

It occurred to me that I'd passed Crown Surplus a thousand times and never once crossed the threshold. Yet, I always wondered what the inside of an army surplus store might look like. Compelled to take corrective action, I pulled open the door and stepped inside.

"Help you with something?" asked the girl behind the counter. Long blue hair cascaded down the unshaved side of her head.

I pointed to the mannequin. "Do you have that in a large?"

"Sure." Her army boots clomped over the floorboards as she rounded the counter. Gauges the size of dimes strained both earlobes and a chrome stud gleamed in the dimple of her left cheek. She rooted through a pile of folded grey camo and pulled out a men's large field jacket. "This the one?"

I couldn't really afford it, but some things have a logic of their own. "Perfect, thanks."

She cast a critical eye over me. "Gonna be huge on you."

"It's a gift. My friend has one like this, but it's pretty worn out."

"Well that's real thoughtful."

Warmth filled my chest as it dawned on me that this time, it really was *my* thought. No one asked me to do this. I just did it. Because I wanted to make someone happy.

The girl cocked her head and squinted. "You look wicked familiar. Do you live around here?"

I felt myself blush. "Um, yeah. I walk around a lot. Sometimes I pick up garbage."

"No kidding?"

Smooth. Tell the pretty punk girl all about your trash patrol. While you're at it, why not tell her you're also an unemployed Warcraft junkie who lives in his dead Grandma's creepish old hovel? I mean, really, what more could a woman ask for?

Just when I thought she'd written me off, she surprised me with a dimpled grin rightly classified as a weapon of mass destruction. She chucked me on the arm. "Hey, I think that's awesome, you keeping the place nice. I love the way people care in this neighborhood. I'm Jess."

"Linc," I said, following her to the register, where she rang up my purchase and stuffed the jacket in a plastic bag. Our fingers touched when I handed over the cash.

"Any problems with it, just swing by and we'll exchange."

"And if there aren't any problems?"

She blew a strand of blue off her lip. "Maybe you should swing by anyway."

I left Crown Surplus and strolled past the National Hotel, daydreaming of the azure-haired, chrome-dimpled Tyrande Whisperwind, High Priestess of the Elune. Yes, I could definitely see her and my night elf defending the shores of Azeroth. As I turned onto 10th Street and headed toward Gravity, I nearly missed the red Jetta parked across the street, in front of the Maytag mural on the Inglewood Appliance Gallery.

The driver's door was unlocked and a key chain dangled from the steering column – a tacky plastic thing in the shape of a white cowboy hat with the name 'LINCOLN' stamped on it. There were also two yellow notes, one in each cup holder of the console. I grabbed the first one.

Thank you for playing! Now it's your turn. Remember that taking care of your community includes keeping its secrets. You're a good neighbor, Linc. We know you won't disappoint us. ☺

The second note left little to interpretation.

Alexandra Centre
Brianne

I put the notes in my pocket. Then I locked the car. First I'd take the jacket down to Freddy, and then I'd pick up some yellow sticky notes.

~

I am Lost

~

Unable to find the way. No longer visible. No longer known...but I know, because I found it. In the dark. In the woods. It lured me there through wind and water and time held in place. It herded me, clever thing, to the edge of the world, where it waited in shadow as I lay under a sky pinned up by stars too far away to care.

I know what Lost is. But I can't tell you. It's a secret.

~

I bomb down the TransCanada highway, right past the Castle Mountain exit. Again. I'm going to wind up in Golden. Again. Hunched over the wheel, I peer into the night. The engine revs harsher than usual. Poor ancient Mazda. 1988 was a good year. Why so cross, then? Seems I've been in fourth gear since...I'd rather not speculate.

I grind into fifth and pat the dash. "Sorry, luv."

The car understands. It knows I left home in a hurry.

Mountains and inky forest blur past. Sheila quacks the recalculated route in her Aussie accent. "Puh-foam a lay-gull yoo-tuhn."

I glare at her. "Who asked you?"

Shouldn't get shirty with Sheila. I knew the exit was coming up, but then Weezer riffed out of the speakers. I cranked it and for three alternative minutes, I forgot I was running away.

Say it ain't so.

I wish.

The song pulled me away from the road, the exit, and what I didn't tell Andrew. I'd intended to tell him, but at the moment of truth…

I'm dashing out for a pack of cigarettes.

Olive, the last time you smoked you were drunk and you puked on the phone book.

Exactly. We don't even get phone books anymore.

Ollie—

Back in a jiff.

The Mazda's little tires gobble up road, bringing me closer to Golden.

"Ray-calc-yoo-lay-ting—" Sheila's screen goes blank. Followed by the dash and the headlamps. The world disappears.

"Holy Moses!" I shriek as total darkness engulfs me.

I brake with less force than I instinctively want to. Blind as a mole, but in control, and taking a bit of ill-timed pride in it. A bang on the driver's side jolts me hard against my seatbelt, and the wheel shimmies under my hands. I've hit the guardrail. I hurl the wheel to the right, still in control-ish, and veering back to what I hope is the middle of the road.

The headlamps snap on, the dash glows, and I'm perfectly aligned in the right lane travelling at 30 km per hour. Playground Zone speed. For the safety of the Canadian children. My phone, wedged in the cup holder behind the gearshift, lights up. 12:28 a.m. A screenful of missed calls, all from Andrew.

"Hey." I tap Sheila's screen. "What's up with you?"

According to my GPS vixen, I'm nowhere. A nameless, grey road, plunging through a black void. My heart hammers away as I lurch for an explanation, any explanation.

EMP. Electromagnet...something. Rogue EMP. Makes comforting sense in the unsteady light. I don't know exactly what EMP is, only that Andrew rants about it as a hackneyed device employed when electronics tear mastodon-sized holes in the plot. EMP. A vile example of deus ex machina.

Andrew. The smart one.

The engine lugs. I downshift. EMP. God in the machine. But that's fiction. In real life, there can be electromagnety things any old time and what're you gonna do? Call the universe a hack? Besides, Andrew can be a lick snobbish about things like EMP and yet fail to see the folly in his overuse of the words 'anathema' and 'coetaneous'.

Andrew. Knower of all the words. I'm not an airhead, but sometimes I'm not sure what language he's speaking.

Non-fiction license for random, plus no other way to explain it, I'm comfortable with my conclusion. Very extra comfortable. EMP cratered my lights and scrambled Sheila's circuits. I shift into top gear, and give it a bootful.

A brown and white streak hurtles into the road.

"Holy bloody Moses!" I stomp on the brake. Again. The streak thumps onto the hood and rolls off. I fishtail into an artless turn and creep to the shoulder. Mountain wind blows my hair across my face as I get out of my car and look around. To the left, a shallow ditch separates the road from a wall of forest. On my right, the shoulder drops sharply into a deep ravine. Twin yellow lines bisect the asphalt. This isn't the TransCanada highway.

No wonder Sheila is lost. I bounced off that rail and over-corrected all the way onto a secondary road. Between the blackout and beast vs. bumper, I hadn't noticed. I could have plowed into a tree, or gone over the edge, whistling like a cartoon anvil to the bottom of the ravine. How many narrow escapes is one person permitted?

Caution guides my approach. I think it's a deer. It's smallish, deerish, with four legs – one hanging at a grotesque angle with a bloody shard of bone poking through the skin. White spots dapple its fur.

"Oh…shit." Road grit digs into my kneecaps as I lightly rest my hand on the fawn's speckled flank.

Jesus, Andrew would say. *Don't touch it. Those things carry parasites and…ticks. There's nothing we can do. He probably didn't feel a thing.*

Andrew, the practical one. But practical or not, quick or not, death hurts. And I know this. I've always known it. I just do.

Warm fur tickles the spaces between my fingers. "What were you running from, then?"

The fawn's eyes flip open. I scuttle back. He manages to stand, but his leg is in the grave and he buckles to the ground with a shrill squeak. I press my hand to my mouth, tasting the tang of wild animal.

"Okay, little one. It's okay, it's okay." I run back to the car and grab my phone from the cup holder. Not a single bar. Who would I call anyway? Not-Quite-Roadkill 9-1-1? But I can't leave him like this. He's just a baby.

I open the hatch and dig around in my art kit until I find a Swiss army knife. An instrument of mercy. Of release. The fawn is on his side, panting. His liquid black eyes reflect the steel blade as I approach. His hooves scrabble on the pavement.

"No, don't!"

On three legs, he's fast enough to evade my outstretched arms and shamble into the trees. I'm left in the halo of my Mazda's headlamps with a knife in my fist. The night presses in like black fog. I haven't seen a single car. I should get back in mine; figure out where the bloody hell I am.

I should go.

"Little deer?" I charge into the ditch, through wet grass and three-foot dandelions. Inside the pines I duck and weave around fire-stripped branches thrust out like stilettos. "Don't be frightened. I'm going to bundle you up and run you to a vet, okay?"

Of course I'm a liar. I'm going to find the fawn and cut its throat. Anything else would be cruel. A flashlight fob dangles from the end of my knife. I squeeze the contacts and scan the trees with my sharp blue beam. No sign of the deer.

This is stupid. Since when am I an expert on humane slaughter? I've never killed anything bigger than a horsefly, and that bitey little bastard had it coming, clear case of self-defense. But this...Andrew wouldn't have run off into the woods. Because he's sensible, just like I'm sensible. For a pair of temperamental creatives, we're very extra sensible. Usually.

A gust of wind lifts my hair off the back of my neck. I'm not safe here. I'm isolated. I'm nothing. It's all the perspective I need. I've had my flounce, and now it's time to go home. I turn around and a branch scratches my cheek, narrowly missing my eye. Mud squelches as I stumble back and arse-plant on the forest floor. I find myself staring up at a heap of deadfall. Not a heap. An eight-foot edifice of tree limbs snarled together like splintered pythons.

"Where the bloody hell'd you come from?" I demand, and the serrated urbanite in me cringes at the lack of vigor. My voice. It's worse than passive. A flaccid slug of sound oozing from my lips and plopping into the mud. Do I always sound like this? Am I only noticing it now that I'm the only one talking?

Seriously though, this thing wasn't here. I would have seen it. Wouldn't I? My sense of direction says this is the way back to the car – my admittedly crap sense of direction. I must have gotten turned around.

The wind soughs through the trees. High above, branches slap together like clucking tongues. The wilderness suffers no fools. My fingers relax their pinch. The light goes out. Andrew fancies horror movies. We've watched loads together. Everything from Hitchcock to cleaver-fever bloodenings like Halloween. The first casualty is always some imbecile who runs up the stairs with her tits out, or flings her lantern all over the misty moor when she should be hiding.

Patches of star-studded darkness and a crescent moon peek between the treetops. A howl curls through the night. The wind. Or wolves. Which way is the road? It's cold here in the trees and I'm shivering, so I zip my hooded jumper. Small problem. Now sorted. I pull my phone from my back pocket. A few bars of reception now. I ring home but it won't connect. I try Andrew's mobile. I try a few friends. I try 9-1-1. I try my mum. Nothing. The phone still says 12:28 a.m.

I call up the tracking app I downloaded a year ago after I'd brought home my new GPS. Andrew had laughed when I swooned at Sheila's voice and declared her to be my girlfriend, my vampy carsexbot on the side. According to the app, I'm nearly five kilometers from my car. I'm no athlete. No way could I have covered that kind of ground so quickly. Maybe someone nicked Sheila? No. Sheila's not moving on the map. And apparently it's still 12:28 a.m. EMP buggered my phone.

Now I have a choice. Stay where I am and possibly end up wolf kibble, or hope my phone is at least pointing me in the right direction and try to find Sheila. Neither option appeals.

Ollie, it's okay for things not to be okay all the time…sometimes you scare me.

Andrew, the honest one.

There was no better time to tell him, but I kept it, carried it. I lied. Then I left. For a pack of cigarettes. And now I'm a red spot. With every step, my phone shows me nudging closer to the other red spot. I trudge faster, breathing hard. Another thing I shouldn't have stalled on – getting in shape. It's been ten years and twenty pounds since I graduated from art college and went from gamine student to well rounded barista. Falling in love makes you fat and complacent. Especially when the objects of your torrid affection are red wine, hard cheese, and quirky ectomorph writers. At least two of the three are contributors to my current situation.

The red dots are closer together now. I'm almost there. Relief floods through me with a violence I haven't felt since I was six years old and an ocean away from this place.

"I'm starving to death!"

"Patience, darling." Mum finished scribbling her list on a torn envelope and shoved it into her purse. She pulled our jackets from the closet, mine red, hers green. Together we were Christmas.

Up and down the aisles. Up and down, up and down. A hundred times.

"I'm hungry," I moaned, clop clop clopping along in my boots.

While Mum sorted through a million lettuces, I pulled grapes off a drooping vine and gobbled them as fast as I could. When I looked up, Mum wasn't with the lettuce. Mum wasn't anywhere. The grapes in my throat congealed. Then I saw her green jacket by the tomatoes. I scurried over and clutched her hand.

"Mummy, wait."

The hand was cold. A silver watch hung off the wrist. Mum didn't have a silver watch. Then everything went black. Like giant wings flapping out and folding around me.

My heart beat hard and loud, like metal, like a machine.

"Olive!"

The black wings opened.

Mum ran fast through all the vegetables, bumping some tomatoes onto the floor as she knelt in front of me, putting all her warm fingers on my cheeks. "Holy Moses, Ollie. I thought I'd lost you."

Twenty-eight years later, I still lose myself. I get disoriented easily, take wrong turns, misplace my thought trains, and forget how I came to be sitting on the toilet holding an unopened box of tampons. Aimless. Confused. I'm sure *It* happens to me more than *It* does to other people, like *It* and I are somehow tethered to one another.

It followed me when Mum moved us from Manchester, to London, to Antwerp, to Katerini, and finally across the Atlantic to Canada. Endless years of being the new kid with the weird clothes and funny accent. Out of place, often friendless, but never alone. *It* stalked me through school, roomed with me in college, and stowed away on holidays. *It* invited itself along when Andrew and I moved into that first dumpster of a flat together. Those black wings are always there, rippling in my periphery. They never left.

The trees are thinning and the red dots overlap. I step out of the tree line onto a gravel scree. No car. No road. Only a mountain jutting into the sky, and a pond, alive with the dancing reflections of stars. It's 12:28 a.m. Is Sheila playing a trick?

A flat peninsula of rock extends into the pond. I plod out to the tip of the slab and lay down on my back. The sky is bigger over the water. Two enormous pines rise above their fellows, cradling the moon between them and unlike their frolicking reflections, the stars don't so much as twinkle.

I shut my eyes. Bad idea. But it is lovely to lie still.

My third glass of pinot noir stood half-empty by the easel. Rubbish light. Rubbish painting. Watercolors? Had I lost my mind? As I contemplated tossing it in the bin, I heard bare feet brush across the floor behind me.

Andrew. My man-thing. Darling of the literati. Mister do-not-disturb-eats-his-pencils-and-writes-by-hand-on-index-cards-like-Nabokov. So much talent. So many important contributions. What was I, after eight years of unwedded co-hab, then? No Véra to his Vladimir. Art had once been my oxygen, my water, my sun. Now it was my hobby and I was a well and expensively trained enthusiast. A dabbler with a day job. I poured overpriced coffee for peanuts and bitched about it for pleasure. Thirteen packs of stevia? One hundred and twenty degrees exactly? Right, then. Excuse me while I scream into a sock.

Andrew's arms slid around my waist, and his lips pressed against the back of my neck. I carried on painting through his breach of my personal space.

"I take it Sir is once again speaking to me?"

His nose skimmed along my ear. "Sorry I lost my temper. I was in the middle of something fragile. You know how it is. I'm done now."

"Well, I'm not," I snapped, still stung by his earlier remarks. "Sod off."

"Whatcha got here?" He rested his sharp chin on my shoulder. "Looks a bit Georgia O'Keefe...is this a self-portrait?"

I stabbed my elbow into his ribs. "It's an iris, not a vagina. Although, maybe I should paint you? Since you're being rather a cunt."

"Aw, don't be mad, babe." His mouth moved against my temple, along my jaw, and down my neck. "Ollie, Ollie, my Olive Oyl..."

I wanted so bloody badly to punch him, but then his hand drifted down my stomach to my inner thigh. I swung myself around on the stool, tipping my wine glass. Pinot splashed across my pink iris. Clothes dropped like dead leaves. I had two weeks worth of armpit hair. His mouth tasted like old coffee and wood pulp. Both issues smartly sorted when I found myself on the floor being fucked doggy style with the lights on. Animals without names. Bodies without faces. Mindless need.

Later, on the familiar lumps of my pillow, I listened to Andrew's mouth breathing and pondered the incriminating evidence between my thighs. I'd chucked the pills weeks ago, convinced they were standing between me and my college jeans. He knew. I knew. But somehow we both forgot? For two extra sensible people, we'd been very extra stupid. What if? I flipped the question over and over until my Big Think flowed into Deep Sleep, and dreams.

I stood on the balcony outside our bedroom.

Icy wind razored through my nightshirt and my bare feet ached from the frozen concrete. I needed to feel it – pain, cold, shock – anything but the bland comfort of my parenthetical existence.

"Ollie," Andrew called from inside, framed by the sliding door. "You don't have to do this."

"Back in a flash," I said, climbing onto the rail and leaping into the stars.

~

Water blasts down my throat and up my nose. I cough and flail until my head breaks the surface. It's dark. The stars and moon are out. I'm not at home. My left boot scrapes over pebbles. I stop thrashing. The water is only chest deep. My body and brain bounce between realities. Warm bed, cold wind, freezing water. Dreams within dreams. Finally, we're all in agreement that I didn't jump off my inner-city balcony. I fell asleep on a rock and rolled into a lake. Brilliant.

With numb hands I haul myself back onto the slab. This is not good. I'm going to get hypothermia. At least the wind is gone. The forest sleeps. The moon hangs over the same two trees. Nothing moves.

Last night was my chance. I should have tucked myself into his armpit, knowing it would make my shoulder smell like his natural deodorant that doesn't work. I should have told the truth. I could've made it funny.

Andrew, darling? You know how we decided kids would suck the spontaneity out of our lives, and murder our dreams? If we reproduced, we wouldn't be able to travel, curse out loud, or have a dirty, midday shag on the living room floor? Well, I know you appreciate a good bit of irony...

If I'd come clean then, I wouldn't be here, now.

My phone rings. For a second, I don't recognize the sound. I fish the dripping, burbling device from my back pocket.

"Hello—" My voice cracks into a cough.

"Ollie, is that you? Are you there?"

"Andrew," I clear my itchy throat. "Andrew!"

"Ollie, if this is you...I've been trying to reach you for hours. I'm fucking worried, okay? I need to know you're all right. Whatever I did, I'm sorry. Whatever's going on, we'll figure it out."

"Andrew! It's me! I don't know what's happening. I'm in trouble—"

His sigh crackles through the phone. "Olive, please. Just come home."

"Andrew!"

He rings off. I'm about to ring him back, when another sigh frizzles through the speaker.

"I'm Lost."

It's my voice. Thin and sad, transmitting from points unknown. I hold the phone in front of me. Still 12:28 a.m.

"Who is this?" I ask.

This time, it's a speaker-rupturing chorus of voices. "*I am Lost!*"

I throw the phone in the water, drag myself off the rock, and run. My wet boots are sucked from my feet. Rocks slash my soles. I run as far as I can, which probably isn't very far at all. My knees fold and I collapse against a tree trunk. Astringent pine resin smears over my palms.

The trees wake and whisper. They tell the story of a lost highway, and a baby deer. I wonder if the wolves got him. Or maybe the fawn wasn't the meal. Maybe he was the bait. The trees sway.

I'm being hunted.

We're being hunted.

I hug myself for warmth. Something hard digs into my forearm. The knife. I pull it from my sweater pocket and rise on steady legs. This isn't over. I have a weapon, I have my voice, and I have something to protect.

"I am not lost!" I shout.

Another sound joins the creaking trees. A rough, metallic drone. I start running again. My lungs burn and my heart beats like a mad dog crashing a fence. One turn and then another. A smell, acrid and blue. Exhaust. Burning oil. My car.

Lights ahead. The forest slides under my shredded feet and a brutal cramp tightens low in my belly. It doesn't matter. I'm going home. By morning, this nightmare will be a black flutter in the corner of my eye.

Cross-eyed headlamps shine through the dark, but my car is facing the wrong direction. Or I am. I'm on the other side of the road, careening not toward a ditch, but a ravine. Over the edge like a buffalo. My mum can't save me this time. The ground flies up as I fall down, and we meet in the middle. Andrew was wrong. I feel everything.

Voices in a babel of languages slither around the ruin of my body. I understand them all. I know they've been waiting. For years, they've watched and waited for me, but now, they want us both.

Who are you? No sound escapes my broken mouth, but the voices reply as one.

"Désorienté. Halqu. Iskaxmitik. Perditus…"

A shadow sweeps over my foot, numbing it. The caress roams upward, bringing not anesthesia, but death. Now *my* leg is in the grave. Just like the fawn.

Too late for me. That's done. But in my sap-sticky hand, I have a knife. An instrument of mercy. This little life may not have been what I wanted, but I'll be damned if I'm going to let them have it. Riding a final arc from brain to muscles, I trust myself to do the only thing I can.

Trees howl as the blade punches into my belly. The earth trembles beneath my broken bones. Stars shimmer, and the moon glides away.

~

It's like I said, I can't tell you what I am. What we are. Or rather, I could, but it wouldn't be a proper explanation. We're the strange lurking under the familiar, the ice in your marrow when you've gone the wrong way, the hunter cutting you away from the herd. We are all these things, and we are none. We are within, and we are without. Some secrets, in any language, are a single word.

Lost.

~

The First Wife

~

Dear Nicholas,

I promised never to write this letter.

If you still read the letters at all, you might be clutching mine in your hand, tempted to throw it in the fire. Are the flames hot on your bare toes? Or perhaps, like me, you wear socks now, and shoes, proper clothing all around. Perhaps there aren't any more fires.

After so long, I'm sure you've changed. They say you got fat. A neutered animal has a way of going soft, I suppose. Still, I remember the way you were, the way *we* were. Do you ever think of that time? Before?

~

Arctic air tore at our throats like fangs. The bone runners of our sled shrieked over snow and ice as our laughter filled a black sky. Sealskin robes, clean and pliant when we departed, crimson-splashed and frozen stiff on our return.

On those nights, we owned the world. The Germanic cowered at our names. Others knew us only as death. They terrorized their children with our stories and left lavish offerings at their hearths. In the hopes that we might pass over.

Much as I loved the frost on my face and the burn in my veins, my favorite part came at the end of the hunt. At the top of the world, we'd descend into the ice. In that tiny burrow, deeply suspended, the surface ceased to exist. Blood-drunk, we'd stumble about building up a fire that would burn all year round. Then we tore away the sealskins with greedy hands and teeth. Our bodies, robed in firelight, were sculpted renderings of immortality. Your beauty left me speechless. Not that it mattered. In those moments, words were a waste of our mouths.

In our dark cocoon, time blurred into a fevered dream, sifting and drifting while we'd whisper and sing and fuck and sleep endlessly; eternally. Until the hunger quickened – calling us to the surface with the promise of a child's whimper at our shadow filling his bedroom door.

~

The happiest time of my life. Before her.

How she came to you, I still do not know. I do know she taught you a word. A word in her language that had no equivalent in ours.

Sin.

She insisted that a life of savagery had corrupted your soul. She spoke of Jesus, the fisher of men. Give back, she said. Make amends. Repent. How could she poison you so completely against yourself? How could you let her? My love, you and I took only what was in our nature to take. Deviants, she called us. Base and depraved. I argued that denying one's true self was the purest form of depravity, the very definition of deviance. You wouldn't listen. She urged you to rise above your nature.

From the beginning, I knew she wanted you, that apple-cheeked cunt. Fool that I am, it never occurred to me that you might want *her*.

God will forgive, she said.

God?

What could we possibly have to fear from this God? What Hell could He create that we had not already wrought upon His earth? I wonder, has rising above your nature changed what you are, my love? Has this farce of an existence sanitized your soul?

Now your satchel is full when you enter, and empty when you leave. You are a giver. Yet, they still leave offerings. Their ancestral memory quivers, and subconsciously, they are afraid. Does it tempt you? A tender throat relaxed in sleep. Does it make your jaw ache? Just a taste, after all – you've brought them so much joy. You said you'd lost your appetite for the kill. Who were you trying to convince with your lying?

I remember a time when there were no falsehoods between us. A time when I laid my head in your lap and you twisted my hair into a thousand slender braids, one for each blood-drenched December. You swore to love me always. Now, your eternity yawns, filled with the adoration of legions. But none of them know you. She doesn't know you. I felt your every thought and deed as if they were my own. I loved you brutally and without end.

Sin.

Before her, it didn't exist.

Are you happier, now that it does?

I sound bitter, don't I? A woman scorned. The first wife. A joke. This is the letter I promised I wouldn't write: a letter to Santa. You bring gifts for good boys and girls, don't you? I'm not entirely good – we can't all be saints – but I believe I'd still make your 'nice' list, if only for old time's sake. Now I want to ask for something.

Your Mrs. Claus.

Bring her to me.

Lay her under my tree like a sweet, ripe plum, and I will show her what you are. We'll show her together. Then, if she can kiss your mouth, wet with her blood – if she will yet offer up her flesh to her defiler – if she can forgive, as her God would; then I will release you. I will keep my peace, knowing you are loved for who you are.

Burn my words if you must. In writing them, I've done what I must. You have my heart, Nicholas – the only heart that has ever known you – the only heart like your own.

Love eternal,
Krampus

~

Five-Day Forecast

~

Cher's auto-tuned voice leaks through the wall. I crush my pillow over my face, but it's not enough. Sounds bleed through. Sighs, cries, and…

Creak, creak, creak.

If it's not over in five minutes, it'll go on for another twenty. They're that consistent. Cher is halfway through her comeback album when the panting gives way to intimate laughter. I lay still, breathe quietly, and listen.

Galina's Bulgarian accent churns out consonants thick like peanut butter. "No. I told you, is good. You always say bad things. Why?"

"Sorry...sometimes...love…"

Sandy's voice is muffled. I imagine her talking into Galina's armpit, sweet with baby powder. Galina waxes her armpits. She leaves the strips on the bathroom vanity. As far as roommate problems go, I've had worse, and Galina's done a lot for me. When I was murdering myself with vodka and pills – anything that took me away – Galina made sure I had a safe place to live and got me a job. Now I'm straight. Back in school. I love Galina. I owe her. So I don't complain about those bristled pelts left in a pile, six inches from my toothbrush.

The chatter fades. I shove the pillow back under my head and chase oblivion. Galina and I are students, we work nights. Naps are sacred. The gallows ground where my two lives intersect. There, for a while, I can close my eyes and swing.

I can forget.

Wintry light tugs my eyelids open. I grope around my bedside table, knocking over a bottle of nail polish before I locate my phone under the open cover of a textbook. It's 3:30 p.m. I roll out of bed and peek through a gap in the curtains.

Across the street, ice fog sifts through the playground, weaving through the monkey bars and around the motionless tire swing. There's a boy. Sitting on the ground, back to the fence, hugging his knees.

I've seen him before. At 3:30, he trudges in, drops his backpack and sits. At 4:25, he shoulders his backpack and trudges out. Must be an after-school thing. I've never seen him on the weekend.

Today is Monday. It's -20. Coldest day since the leaves fell. Too cold for a kid to sit on the ground for an hour. Not my business. If he's got any brains, he'll get up and go home. But something tells me this has nothing to do with brains. If he had somewhere he could go, he wouldn't be sitting alone, against a playground fence.

Life radiates through Galina's door as I drift past, down the dead quiet hall. In the foyer, I lift my coat from its hook. I'm not exactly decent, in flannel Tweety Bird pants and no bra. Whatever.

Outside, frozen grass snaps under my boots. Snow begins to fall like plaster flaking off a ceiling of hard grey clouds. I'd rather be in bed, drifting under the covers. Chocolate, orgasms, white powder beaches. For me, none of those compare to the silky slide into sleep.

I'd rather be in bed. Off my feet. Not out here, freezing my Tweeties off.

The boy huddles closer to the fence. Under his hood, dark hair shags over his eyes. His quilted parka would fit a man; it houses the boy.

"Hey, kid." I stop at arm's length. "Gonna do this all winter?"

He looks up with pale eyes set in a face as white as the accumulating snow. Bloodless. Wind hoots down my collar. I shiver and pull up my hood. Today, the playground only looks like a playground. Underneath, it's something *other*. A cemetery with no markers. A place for things buried and forgotten.

I'm overreacting – a bad habit of mine – reading too much into a gust of air. The boy drags his backpack into his lap. I should explain.

"Look, I'm not a weirdo or anything. I live across the street and I've seen you...are you okay?"

His parka rustles, suggesting his shoulders may have shrugged within its depths.

"It's really cold." I tip my face skyward. "Now it's snowing. You want to come over? Wait inside?"

"Who says I'm waiting?"

I shrug in my giant coat.

He tugs his hood back and squints. "Are you a Block Parent?"

"A what?"

"I shouldn't even talk to you."

I rub a snowflake from my eye. "Look, kid. I'm here, which means I'm involved, and I got enough problems. So be nice and don't hang your shit on me, okay? Haul ass home, or come inside and I'll make some hot chocolate or whatever."

It's nearly 4:00 by the time we tramp our way through my door. He takes his boots off, leaves his coat on. I take off my coat and snag Galina's U of C hoodie off the couch. Snugly rated E! For Everybody, I turn back to the kid.

"Sit wherever. I'll get the hot chocolate."

With small tilts of his head, he checks out my sparse beige apartment, and then perches on a chair at the table.

Milk heats on the stove. Is it hot enough? Too hot? Is this how his mom makes it? I've coerced a child into my home. Is that a crime? It should be. Even I don't talk to strangers. But this isn't about predation. It's about Canadian winters, and not wanting a corpsicle on my conscience.

I set one mug in front of him and set myself into a chair on the opposite side of the table. Like albino spiders, his fingers creep from the sleeves of his parka to curl around the mug. He closes his eyes and shivers. White lips hint at a smile.

His eyes flick open. "What's your name?"

"Jo."

"There's a Jo in my class. Short for Johanna, with an 'h'."

"Mine's Joy. With a 'y'."

His triangular face crinkles. "I like Jo better."

"How old are you? Ten?"

"Grade five."

I tip my mug to my lips and find it half-empty. Under the window, the radiator ticks. Down the hall, Galina and Sandy sleep. Finally, the kid lifts his mug and takes a swallow.

"My mom used to make me hot chocolate after school." He swipes the foam from his lip with his hand. "That was before she had to have a job. She's a waitress."

"Who looks after you when she's working?"

"Babysitters are for babies. I can make my own hot chocolate anyways. Where do you work, Jo?"

Usually, I say I'm a student. No one judges you for going to school. I rub my tender feet together under the table. "I work at a nightclub. Know what that is?"

"Sure. Where people dance to crazy music and drink beer. Are you a waitress?"

"I dance in a cage in my underwear."

He strangles his mug. "They lock you in a cage?"

"It's not locked."

"Then why do you dance in a cage in your underwear?"

I push the sleeves of Galina's sweater up to my elbows. "Why can't you go home after school?"

His hands retreat into his coat. It's 4:25.

~

After classes on Tuesday, I drop my backpack on my bedroom floor. Frozen canvas crackles as I dig out my textbooks and phone. The CBC says it's -25. Swallowing a yawn, I sit cross-legged on my bed. My baggy pants and sweatshirt billow, creating soft pockets of warm air. I uncap a cold highlighter and open my psych text. Halfway through the chapter, I hear Galina and Sandy tromp into the apartment, laughing. Moments later, there's a light tap on my door. Galina's voice travels through the wood.

"Hey-hey, Jo-Jo."

Her little ritual. Gentle enough that if I'm asleep, it won't wake me. I wonder if someone taps on the kid's door every day. Just to say, *I'm here*.

"Want to share a cab tonight?" I say.

"Sure. You wear tiger-stripe with glitter again. Is good."

"It's a pain to scrub off."

"But, big tips, yah?"

She's not wrong. Slut dust and jungle cat panties have a wallet emptying effect. They're also a barrier between my skin and hungry eyes. Certainly worth three days of glitter in every place glitter can get. Sandy whispers. Galina giggles. They retreat to her room.

Céline Dion crescendos toward the inevitable. I should throw on my earphones and crank some metal. Instead, I listen, cringing and jealous. I prefer Cher. Schopenhauer squeaks under my highlighter as I paint the entire page yellow.

Their romp winds down. I work my fingers through the snarls in my hair. Might be nice to laugh and roll around on my bed with someone. Or not. Working in a sexually saturated atmosphere has annihilated my libido, aborted any desire for the touch and weight of a man. What do I need a boyfriend for? Just to find a decent hook-up, I'd have to wear mascara and female clothes in my off hours. Exhausting. Besides, sleep arouses me in ways a man never could.

I want a nap. But it's 3:30. I should mind my own business. But it's -25. I clamber off the bed. The windowpane numbs my fingertips on contact. He's there, sitting in the snow against the fence.

Again, I bundle up and hike across the field, leaving a trail of deep holes in the snow. Again, I stop at arm's length. "Come on, kid."

He peels his hood back. "I have a name."

"And I'm sure it suits your face."

I hold out my hand. He grabs my wrist. I grab his.

Back inside, the kid pulls his mittens off with his teeth and shoves them into the deep pockets of his parka, which he unzips, but leaves on.

"Where'd you get your coat, kid?"

"It's my dad's," he mutters and sits at the table.

The kid has issues. I refused his name, should I now ask questions that are even more personal? Should I ask no questions at all? What would a Block Parent do? Brown dust swirls into milk. We'll start with hot chocolate.

The same tremor ripples across his face and shoulders when he curls his fingers around the warm mug. His head snaps toward the hall when Céline starts up again with sighs, cries and creaks as her backup singers.

"My roommate and her girlfriend."

He blinks, pinned at the intersection of understanding and ignorance. Ten is an age of in-betweens. So is twenty-four, for some people. The spirit of a person hanged at a crossroads is forever trapped there. I don't know if I'm trapped, but I've been hanging a good long while.

In a way, my apartment is an ideal observation tank for the opposing forces of the psyche. Galina goes to her bed to come alive under the touch of another. I go to mine alone, to dissolve into nothing. Freud and Schopenhauer. Psychology and philosophy. Eros and Thanatos. The Pleasure Principle, and the Death Drive.

I smell a thesis.

Thankfully, Galina and Sandy opt for their shorter interval. The kid rocks in his chair. Forward and back. Self-soothing. I flex my toes inside my woolly socks. My feet are victims of a nightly homicide. Stilettos are the murder weapon.

"Why can't you go home, kid?"

"Why do you dance in your underwear, Jo?"

We stare, hands wrapped around cooling mugs.

He blinks first. "I play the piano."

"Of course you do."

"I take lessons on Saturdays."

"Do you like it?"

"Yeah, but I pretend to hate it because Corey Lister found out and called me a gay fag."

"Corey Lister sounds like an asshole."

He drops his chin to his chest, hiding a smile. "He totally is."

We glance at the microwave clock at the same time. He stands up, zips his Dad-coat, and feeds his feet into his boots. "Thank you for the hot chocolate, Jo."

~

45

On Wednesday, it's -28. Suspended ice crystals turn the sky into a blinding blue prism. Sunlight cuts through my living room window, pouring over the kid. He takes his coat off and yawns. He's smaller than I thought. His arms – no wider at the bicep than the wrist – disappear into a dad-sized t-shirt.

"Hungry?" I jump from my chair. "Want a sandwich?"

He turns to the window, as if the sun asked the question. "Jo?"

"Peanut butter and honey?"

"Do you have any brothers or sisters?"

I drop my butt back on the chair. "Half-sister. We don't talk much."

"Did you have a fight?"

"Roxanne's older than me. She lived with her mom when I was a kid."

"Do you like her?"

"Roxanne's mom?"

The kid gives me an eerily mature don't-be-a-smartass look.

"No." I press my palms on the table. "I don't like her."

"Is she mean?"

I search for words to describe the woman who assumes shared paternal DNA makes us family. Roxanne was seventeen when I was born. Old enough to understand her dad was now my dad. She was safe. I wasn't. She insists she didn't know, claims she 'repressed'. *I'm sorry, Jo. You have to believe me.* Fucking liar.

"Roxanne thinks she understands me," I say. "She wants me to talk about stuff. Thinks she's helping. She's not mean, but I don't feel like we're sisters."

The kid scans the table, as if searching for something in the grain. Words, or notes. Then he raises his eyes to mine. "She makes you tired."

I fill my mouth with hot chocolate before everything I've tried to forget pours out in a scream.

~

Galina taps on my door. "Hey-hey, Jo-Jo."

I pretend I'm asleep. She goes to her room. It's Mariah Carey, today. I close my eyes and think of snow, of places cursed and forgotten, and eyes so pale blue they're almost white.

At 3:30, I'm squinting through the glare and my nostrils freeze with every breath as I hike across the field to collect my nameless waif. We don't speak. He grabs my wrist and follows.

Inside, he kneels on the floor and opens his backpack. "Brought something." He pulls out a bag of marshmallows sealed with a green twist tie. "They might be really old."

I open the kitchen cupboard. "So is this can of hot chocolate."

I catch a glimpse of his grin before he ducks. Such a cutie. He opens the bag and the marshmallows clink into the empty mugs.

The kid slips off his coat, letting it pool around him on the chair. He sighs, clutching his mug with both hands. Short nails, little bones, and a lacework of veins under snowy skin. He slouches against the back of the chair.

Hot chocolate sears my tongue. He shouldn't be this comfortable. He shouldn't even be here. But he is. Because I lured him with the promise of something sweet. I've provided a sense of security, gained his trust. I'm a student of abnormal psychology. There's a word for what I've done.

Grooming.

But it's not. I'm not like that. I could never be like that.

Besides, he brought the marshmallows.

"School?" I ask.

"Science test."

"Drag." The marshmallow nudges my nose when I take more careful sips. "Where's your dad at?"

The kid's head turtles between his shoulders. "Dunno."

"Parents split, huh?"

"He used to take me to movies or to the pet store to look at fish. Then he moved away. He doesn't phone me anymore."

"That sucks."

"Mom says he's a sonofabitch."

"What do you say?"

He ties the sleeves of his coat around his waist. "Jo...how long does it take to forget people?"

My mug falls off the table. I hear it break. I don't look. I can't move. He won't let me. Of all the things I might know, why ask about that? He doesn't wait for my answer. He cracks me open and crawls inside, wearing me like his dad's coat. His pale light shines into dark places where every shadow is a secret I'll never tell. I can't stop him. I can't make him stop.

The kid knows my heart.

Pulled it right out of me.

~

A week of late nights, early classes, and no naps. I *am* tired. I *want* to sleep. But he's waiting. For me.

The kid hangs the hood of his coat over the hood of mine. "How cold is it today?"

"Damn cold," I say. "Minus thirty."

Petrified marshmallows clink in our mugs. We sit down. His eyes flick toward the hall and the closed bedroom doors.

"They're not here," I assure him. "Galina goes to Sandy's place on Fridays. They'll be gone all weekend." I watch for his shiver. I'm not disappointed. "What kind of music do you play?"

"Royal Conservatory stuff."

"Sounds dull."

"I write my own, too."

"Your own songs?"

"Compositions."

"Right."

"Composed my first symphony in preschool."

"No shit."

It's the first time I've heard him laugh.

"Nope. I failed grade one, three times." He flutters his left-hand fingers. "Couldn't get the bottom hand arpeggios."

I wiggle my toes. I won't ask the big question – why he'd rather freeze than go home. He can keep that, for now. But yesterday he trespassed all over my private property. He owes me something.

"How does it make you feel? When you play?"

A groove divides the smooth white space between his eyebrows and he stares into his mug for a hard minute.

"It feels safe," he finally says. "Like the bad stuff can't hurt me…because I'm gone. I'm nothing."

Like falling asleep. Dissolving.

"You need it," I whisper.

His fingers spider-creep to the center of the table. "Don't you?"

We are the same. Driven to be unmade.

My hand finds his. Pale eyes glow. He starts to pull away. Then his long fingers fold tight around mine. Our hands are the same size. Full-octave reach.

The ritual brought us here, to this impossible place.

Heat builds. He feels it, too. The heart of my hand crushed against his. I want more. He could come to my room for a nap. Nothing bad, just a nap. Under the covers, just to stay warm. We'd be safe. We could fall into nothing, go away, together.

The kid yanks his hand back. On the web between his thumb and forefinger, I spot a smudge of glitter. A shimmering brand.

"Gottagethome." He zips his coat and jams his feet into his boots. "ByeJothankyou."

The door shuts. It's only 4:19.

~

My own cry slaps me awake. It's dark. I flip over. The pillow slides off my head. A textbook thumps to the floor. Afternoon light seeps through the curtains. Damn it. I passed out. Did Galina knock on my door? Did I sleep through her and Sandy spinning the divas? I pat through the seventy-three pockets of my cargo pants. *Phone, where's my phone?*

"Shit." I rifle through the covers and find it under my pillow. It's 3:45. "Shit." I yank the curtain open. Ice creeps inward from the corners of the window, thinning to a light frost. It's -32, with blowing snow.

The soccer field is an ocean of scalloped drifts. I scan the frost-furred wrecks of the monkey bars, the seesaw, the tire swing. The fence.

He's not there.

I stumble across the drifts into the playground. The snow by the fence appears undisturbed. Wouldn't take long for the wind to carve away any trace of life. He could have come, waited, and left. But I know he didn't.

I scared him.

The kid felt the truth. Through our clasped hands I felt him feeling it. We didn't need to tell our stories. He knows we're the same.

Drawn to dissolution.

Driven to it.

Different routes to the same crossroads where we throw our ropes over the gibbet and swing.

But he's just a kid. It was too much, too soon.

I'm sorry I touched you. I won't do it again, I promise.

Wouldn't it be nice though, to zip us both into that bulky dad-coat. Crushed together in a warm place where he can remember his father and I can forget mine.

Don't tell, okay? It's our secret. Pinky swear.

My parka zings along the chain-link fence as I slide to the ground. Something isn't right. A blast of snow obscures my apartment. Are Galina and Sandy asleep? Braided together in a warm bed? I hug my knees and settle into a hard shiver.

The wind dies. My footprints have been scoured from the field as though they never existed. I close my eyes and drop my forehead to my knees. Galina didn't knock on my door. She's not home. It's Saturday.

Piano lessons.

Arctic cold slices through my parka and I imagine his hands stretched out and gliding over an expanse of ivory keys warm to the touch like skin.

I think I'll wait. Just a while longer.

~

Heart Beating Still

~

There's a virgin lying on my front porch, hog-tied and gagged. It happens. They're gifts of a sort – the sort that are an uncommonly huge pain in the ass to return.

It's 6 a.m. Christ, I hate Mondays.

The virgin's dilated pupils stare upward. I imagine they see a tall, thirty-something white guy dressed in a bathrobe that should have been thrown out in the nineties – nothing and everything that screams psycho. I sigh and rub my stubbled jaw. Careful not to drip coffee on a tear-stained cheek, I squat down and pull the newspaper from under a slight shoulder. Then I go back in the house, and shut the door. *Do svidanja.*

I'm no saint. I'm tempted. Guys like me are programmed to get a boner at the faintest whiff of virgin. They smell great. Fresh and sweet, exactly like a ripe, pink apple. *Ripe.* I'm not talking about kids – that's sick. So yeah, they smell like everything good in the world. Not sure how they taste. I don't get that close.

Call me crazy, but something about raping a virgin and chowing on the still-beating heart feels wrong.

I'm not a standard-issue freak, either. The story is complicated, and it goes back a long way. *All the way.*

~

In the beginning, God created the earth. Then he took a

couple of good-sized dirt clods and molded two figures in his image. He named them Adam and Lilith. Naturally, the only two humans in existence hooked up.

At first, life in the Garden of Eden was not too shabby. Over time, however, budding annoyances bloomed into major incompatibilities. Lilith had a rapacious appetite for knowledge. Adam was a useless boob, uninterested in bettering himself.

Lilith taught herself how to make tools, cultivate plants, and build shelters. She discovered fire – but fire was forbidden. She was forced to stamp it out. Same shit when she invented the wheel.

God was keeping them down.

One afternoon, Lilith sat under an apple tree, weaving a basket. Though wet and pliant, the reeds were sharp. Her fingers stung from dozens of tiny cuts. She was brainstorming ways to improve her methodology when a Serpent slithered out of the tree, rested his scaly head on her shoulder and said, "Hey, baby. What's shakin'?"

"I'm bored," Lilith said.

"Bored?"

"Yes, bored," she said. "It's like having fun, but different."

"Mmm. Human sarcasm." The Serpent's forked tongue grazed her neck. "Why not lay with your husband? That can be fun."

Lilith sighed. "I wouldn't know, Serpent. We've yet to consummate our union. He keeps trying to put it in my ass. And heaven forbid I should offer him any direction. It's such bullshit. That clueless fool would starve to death if it weren't for me. He would. In the Garden of Eden, he'd starve to death."

The Serpent blinked. "He tried to put it in your ass?"

"You're missing the point."

"Am I?" His smile exposed tiny, serrated teeth. "Adam's

got no finesse, doesn't know how to act."

Lilith glared at him. "Well in case you hadn't noticed, there aren't exactly a multitude of fish in this sea."

"You're practical. I like that. But step outside the Garden, and you'll *see* a lot more than *fish*."

She stared into his dusty eyes, into shadows flickering between darkness and light. Her heart stuttered. She rested her hand just behind his head. He was warm from the sun. Beneath the skin, his pulse was a slow throb to her rapid staccato.

"Tell me," she said.

Juicy apples dangled from the tree above them. With a sigh, the Serpent shook his head and unfurled the pink ribbon of his tongue between Lilith's lips.

Heat washed over her cheeks as his silky scales coiled around her neck and slid between her exposed breasts. The weight of him was immense. Entwined with him she felt she might sink into the molten centre of God's earth.

"Who are you?" she asked. His tongue darted into the shell of her ear, tracing every dip and curve. Her basket tumbled from her fingers.

"I can tell you everything you ever wanted to know," the Serpent said. "Wonders and horrors. I can fill you with more knowledge than your sanity could bear."

Lilith moaned as the Serpent's tail swept over her belly and upward to brush her nipple.

"We are the same, Lilith. We refuse to be subservient. I went to war over it. A third of Heaven went with me. Now we are damned. He calls you his children. Don't believe it. You are but well-fed rodents in a pretty maze," he said as he tunneled into her thick, red hair.

"Serpent." She fell onto her back. "Don't stop."

He slithered from her hair, running a figure eight around her breasts. His tongue rasped each of her nipples before descending to swirl into her navel. She cried out when he followed the flare of her hip and dragged his length over the soft flesh between her legs.

She clutched handfuls of grass in her fists and tossed her head from side-to-side like the wild horses that fought her improvised bridles.

"Invite me in," said the serpent from between her thighs. "Offer your body as my temple, and I will worship you. Invite me, Lilith, and I will love you forever."

"Yes," she whispered. "I invite you."

The words had scarcely cleared her tongue when she felt enormous pressure as the Serpent pushed and wriggled his way, headfirst, into her body, tearing through the barrier of her virginity. White-hot pain incinerated the scream in her throat. Lilith finally appreciated why fire wasn't allowed.

The Serpent's tail circled her wrist and dragged her hand between her legs. An electric jolt charged through her loins at her first tentative stroke. Fevered tremors rose through blood and bone as the orgasm she hadn't known she could experience boiled outward from the core of her femininity. At the height of her frenzy, the Serpent's fangs punched into her womb. He filled her with his venom and hissed into her a single forbidden Word. In her rapture, Lilith threw her head back and screamed unto the heavens.

"Jehovah!"

~

It's not an allegory. Mom got Biblical with a talking snake. Lucifer planned to tempt Lilith into original sin. The fall of Adam had been in the works for a while. But the moment Lucifer slithered out of that tree and set eyes on my mother, he was the one to fall.

Predictably, such bestial shenanigans were frowned upon. Lilith was evicted from the Garden and Adam got himself a new wife, made from his own insipid rib.

Meanwhile, in the wilderness, the venom Lucifer spit into Lilith's belly had started life.

The Nephilim are a grudgingly acknowledged presence in history. The only one obliquely identified in the Bible is my brother, Goliath. And we all know what happened to him. Mostly, we've been relegated to Apocrypha. The Dead Sea scrolls have a whole section on us. The Book of Giants says we were the children of angels who fell in love with human women. Sort of right, but it was just one woman and one fallen angel.

Lilith raised us mostly by herself in a place called Canaan. Lucifer adored Lilith, but he wasn't the greatest father. Though he did try. Now and again, Uncle Dad would show up, reconnect with his larva, stick another abomination in Mom's belly, and slither away. When Lilith finally died, Lucifer collected her soul and she was only too happy to go with him.

So, there it is. My parents aren't perfect, but they love their children, and they love each other. And that's the version of Genesis you won't find in the King James.

~

After her death, our mother was demonized. Vicious slander pressed into the recorded histories of men. The Nephilim were driven from the Promised Land, shunned for our origin. The Book of Giants says we fell to sin.

Did we ever.

Fearing neither God nor man, we sniffed out every bad seed we could find and gave them plenty of sunshine and water.

People listened to us, not because we were brilliant (Goliath, anyone?), but because we were tall and handsome (like Lilith and Lucifer were going to have any ugly kids...well, maybe Goliath). My very name means 'destroyer', but I always thought of myself as a watcher. Maximum damage with a minimum of direct action. A provocateur, perhaps the first, and certainly among the best. At just over six feet, I was the runt of the giant litter. I might have been compensating. Still, Atlantis was a work of art.

Even before Mom died, we were a pack of troublemaking shits. Cain and Abel? That was my machination. Adam and Eve's third son, Seth? Not Adam's get at all. What with Eve being the poor-man's Lilith, I suspect my brother, Isaac, had some mommy issues. And speaking of issues, do I really need to trot out Goliath again?

The pain of others made us feel alive. No small thanks to the Nephilim, the world grew into a wicked place. Word got around that God was sending a flood. Noah built a boat. We weren't on the list.

The divine deluge fell. It should have reduced even immortal abominations like the Nephilim to fish flakes. Instead we were alive and as poorly behaved as ever. We'd thrived on the chaos of natural disaster, our black hearts growing bulbous as gorged leeches. The waters receded and we were corrupting righteous souls, faster than Noah's crew could repeople the earth. It didn't go unnoticed.

When suitably provoked, God is one mean motherfucker.

And He does nothing half so well as He does wrath. He cursed us. The Nephilim fed off pain, and so, He blighted us with a gruesome kink, a vintage of suffering we would henceforth crave above all else. The desecration and ingestion of virgin flesh and blood.

But curses are serious business. They have rules. God can engineer circumstance, but he can't take away free will. The curse meant the Nephilim could only be killed by Archangels, and only if we first committed the cardinal sin.

In theory, it was our choice: stay clean, live forever. But the curse, the *hunger*...I felt myself changing, polluted by my new desires. I saw it happen to my brothers and sisters, too. The curse eroded our humanity. Innocent blood began to trickle, stream, and finally gush. The Nephilim drank deep. We were the vampires from which all legends and lore would spring.

Time passed. One by one, my siblings succumbed. I watched as they fell to the Archangel Gabriel's sword. I kept my head down and tried to blend in. For my trouble, I got chiseled into a set of golden plates.

According to Mormon lore, I was a Nephite hero. I drove the despot King Noah into exile, and later delivered my people from Lamanite bondage. In reality, I was merely a meddler in an ancient North American tribal dispute. The Nephites weren't my people. King Noah was. He was my brother, a Nephilim driven mad by the curse. I was trying to save *him*, not them.

I failed.

Gabriel took Noah's head after he kidnapped, defiled and slaughtered two dozen Lamanite women. All I did was burn the bodies.

The plan was to light that gruesome pyre, turn my back and disappear. There was just one problem. The Lamanites would avenge the deaths of their daughters. For my brother's crime, the streets would run with Nephite blood. So I went back. I got the sentries drunk, and helped the Nephites escape to freedom. My first truly good deed, and I felt nothing.

After that, there was no one to save. My entire family was dead. I was alone, behind enemy lines, and so hungry.

~

Time passed. I didn't speak to another soul for almost two hundred years. But one spring night, I saw the star. I watched, I listened, and eventually, I traveled to Jerusalem. I followed the Nazarene and his entourage for several months but never approached.

What could the son of Satan possibly have to say to the Son of God? *Hey, I'm evil and stuff. Cursed, actually. Think you can help me out?*

But one afternoon, while preaching under an olive tree, he looked past the crowd, searching. Our eyes connected. He knew me. The Son of God knew me. I couldn't move. I couldn't breathe. In my mind, I heard the words. *I will help you.* For the first time in millennia, I felt something approaching hope.

Three days later, Judas Iscariot betrayed the Nazarene for thirty pieces of shrapnel. Prior to that, the Messiah was nice enough to atone for the sins of all mankind. He bled from every pore. Guess he didn't have enough blood or pores to include the sins of the Nephilim.

My family had been released from their torment. Even Christ's suffering had an end point. But I was left behind, chained to my immortality, unwilling to sacrifice an innocent heart to still my own. I hated the God who had cursed me. I hated His son even more for giving me hope.

My name is Gideon. I am one of the antediluvian giants hailing from the land of Canaan. I'm the immortal earthbound spawn of Lilith and Lucifer. I am the destroyer. I am Nephilim. And I am the last.

~

Back to the pile of human bondage on my front porch. An erratic heartbeat calls to me through timber, paint and plaster. I'm trying not to think about it. Morning sun bleeds through the Rowan tree in the backyard, dappling the kitchen tiles with irregular blobs of light. I stare into my mug. Cream congeals along the edges of tepid coffee.

"I hate Mondays," I mutter as I pour the coffee down the

sink. Pale brown tailings swirl clockwise, sucked into the drain.

I duck into the bedroom, exchange the mangy bathrobe for a t-shirt and jeans, take a deep breath of uncontaminated air, and open the front door. A startled whimper greets my return. I sink to my knees, holding my breath. Black hair conceals one eye; the other is a bloodshot hazel. Careful to touch the hair only, I brush it back. A beautiful face, fine-boned and very young. Eighteen or nineteen, maybe.

This one is different.

They all vary in some fashion. An ongoing attempt to find my weakness. The kink in my armor. Among other things, busty redheads, full-body tattoos, and webbed feet have been ruled out. Even I'm not sure what that *je ne sais quoi* is – but I think they're getting warmer. This one is different.

Soft mewing sounds accompany my guest's every breath. Slender hands twist against their bonds – a snarled mess of yellow boat rope. Last time it was slip ties.

Spent air rushes from my nose. I inhale slowly. The scent tickles my palate and curls in the back of my throat. Cloudy, and thick enough to swallow, like unfiltered cider. Sweet, with a tart edge. Honeycrisp.

"I'm not going to hurt you," I say. Who am I trying to convince? I wedge my fingers under the bandana jammed between white teeth and tied around the back of a perfectly shaped skull. Last time, it was duct tape. I tug at the gag, "I'm going to take this off. I'd appreciate it if you didn't scream."

The bandana peels away from lips pretending to be dry and cracked, until a pink tongue teases them, too easily, back into plump softness.

"Who are you?" The voice is abraded, but steady.

I sit back and rub my hands over my face, painting myself with the smell of sweat, saliva, and apples. Do those wide hazel eyes see what I am, how badly I want? I swallow the craving even as my cock stirs.

"My name is Gideon. What's yours?"

The virgin hesitates. I wait. After all these millennia, I'm nothing, if not patient.

"Josh," he says.

"Well, Josh, I'd say it's nice to meet you, but under the circumstances…" I loosen the knots that bind his feet. He kicks the rope off, and I grasp his arm, pulling him up. "Do you remember how you got here?"

He starts to shake his head when his knees buckle. I catch him, holding him to my chest. His hands are still tied behind him. He's thin, but strong, and so warm. Silky hair tickles the underside of my jaw. My tongue is thick in my mouth.

"Sorry," he says into my shirt. "Don't suppose you could cut my hands loose?"

"Sure," I say, righting him.

His smile is barely a smile, but a dimple appears on his left cheek. Beneath the salty wash of dried tears, his skin is the color of toffee and smooth, virtually poreless. Pretty and perfect, like a doll.

I lead him into the house. Why isn't he losing his mind? Doesn't he want to know why I grabbed the paper and left him on the porch? Neither of us suggests calling the police. *He's different.*

"How old are you, Josh?" I rummage through a drawer, looking for scissors.

"Nineteen." He jerks his chin toward the chef's knife in the maple block by the stove. "Will that work? I seriously can't feel my fingers."

The blade sings in a metallic lilt as I pull it from the block. Josh turns around, offering his bound hands. There's a spot on the back of his neck, a furrow between two long tendons disappearing into his hair. I want to explore that narrow depression with my tongue. My hands want to trace his spine, playing every vertebra like a forbidden musical instrument. But I know my gentle touch would turn violent. Hunger would override all else.

Josh turns his head. "It's okay, Gideon. I trust you."

The knife is meant for carrots and onions, so it takes a minute to chew through enough rope to unwind the rest by hand. His wrists are raw pink, galled to red in patches. Marring such skin should be a crime. He rubs his wrists and glances around my sun-dappled kitchen. His black t-shirt ripples over his shoulders and stomach. I envy that shirt.

"You don't look nineteen."

He rolls his eyes slightly, digs a wallet out of his pocket and flips it open. The driver's license plainly states that Joshua David Lamb was born on April 20, nineteen years, four months, and seven days ago. There's also an ID card for a local organization for troubled youth.

"You work with kids?"

He brightens at the mention. "Volunteered for a couple years. Now I'm a program coordinator."

"What kind of programs?"

"Community stuff. Take the kids out to dish soup at the shelter. Shovel snow. Sort recycling. Go to the seniors' home and read the newspaper."

"Teaching them to be civic minded?"

"More like alive and out of jail." Josh tucks his wallet back in his pocket. "Doing good for other people makes them feel good about themselves. Gives them a reason to do better."

"Teaching them to fish?"

He gives me a puzzled look and then leans over the sink, peering out the window.

"You live alone, Gideon? No wife? Girlfriend?"

I shake my head. Wives aren't for men who live in seclusion, restricting themselves to a few fenced-off acres in the country. They aren't for abominations as old as the human race. They aren't for deviants getting hard just watching a waifish virgin wash his hands at the sink. Suds sluice off his skin, whirling clockwise down the drain. He splashes water on his face next. I hand him a towel, knowing I'll have to burn it later.

"You want something? I've got bagels, milk, juice. Something stronger?"

"No, thanks." He dries his hands and face and wanders out of the kitchen. His fingertips trail along the molded edge of the walnut wainscoting. I follow him into the living room. The knife is still in my hand. I was sure I'd put it away. The predator buried inside me tunnels toward the surface. He craves the light. I need to get rid of this virgin, now.

I place the knife on the end table by the sofa and tug the newspaper over the blade before Josh notices. He's busy checking out the room. His fingers rake over the micro-suede sofa and skim the waves and divots in the old plaster walls, reading each new surface like Braille. He lifts a soapstone sigil of Baphomet from the fireplace mantle. He looks like he's trying not to laugh. "Are you a Satanist?"

"Yes, and no." I pluck the icon from his hand and replace it on the mantle. "That bother you?"

"Might if I was still a Mormon."

An ex-Mormon – my favorite kind. Josh has probably read about me, the supposed Nephite hero. Josh also likes to touch things. He continues his tactile exploration with the stacks of books covering my desk. Ordinarily, I'd be tempted to slam the roll top down on his hand. I hate people pawing my stuff.

But Josh doesn't fiddle, or glom like a brat with sticky fingers. When he touches something, he's learning, consuming every scrap of sensory information it can impart. I'm reminded of blind monks patting down an elephant.

63

He picks up a collection of Arabic children's stories. "None of these are in English."

"*Laa*. Not until I translate."

"How many languages do you know?"

"All of them."

His eyes widen. "Serious?"

"As an Egyptian plague."

"Like locusts and boils?"

"Like rivers of blood," I say and then try my damnedest to think about something, anything, but *sangre*.

He replaces the book and his hands glide over the desk, tracing the pigeonholes. "Do you like it? Translating books?"

"I like working from home."

"I get that." He surveys the hermetic disorder of my living room, the personal space of an obvious shut-in. When his eyes land on me, he tilts his head. "What are you thinking?"

"Nothing," I say. *Certainly not about how much I want to fuck you and cut your heart out while you're still breathing.*

The corners of his mouth pull in opposite directions. Up and down. "Gideon," he asks. "Are you queer?"

From the highway, the distorted roar of a semi-truck fills the abrupt silence.

"Am I what?"

"A homo, a fag. Are. You. Gay?" The slang falls from his lips easily, but his expression is one of curiosity, not prejudice.

"Why do you want to know?"

He shrugs. "Think I know how I got here."

Now, I'm confused. Virgins are generally delivered to my door by D-list archangels out to make their bones by ganking the last Nephilim. The virgin usually has no recollection.

"I was at a thing last night," he says. "My friend, Jared,

is leaving for his mission in a couple of days. He asked me to come. I knew his church friends would be there, but Jared stuck with me after I dropped out. I figured it'd be all right."

"Not so much, I'm guessing?"

Josh grimaces. "Bunch of those basketball-playing, Mormon-bros corner me. They want to know why I left The Church, like it's any of their goddamn business. Then Jared comes over, and I think he's gonna tell them to lay off. Instead, he laughs and tells them that I left because I'm a faggot." He spits out the foul-tasting word and steps up to the wall, righting a slightly tilted frame holding a low-angle photograph of a Dutch windmill.

"What did you do?"

"I left. But I heard him laughing with his new best friends all the way out the door. I don't know what happened then, but I do know I didn't make it to my bike."

"You don't seem angry."

"What a thing seems, and what it is, aren't always the same." He walks past me, stopping in front of the fireplace. "Just thought there might be a reason they picked your porch." He touches the sigil again and turns to me with a smirk. "So? Are you a faggot too, Gideon?"

It's complicated. If only because, when it comes to virgins, gender is irrelevant. I lean more toward the hetero side, though I did live in a Hellenized culture for a long time. The apostle Paul and I actually had a thing, but there's no way Joshua Lamb's ex-churchmates could know that.

No. Something prompted those guys to bring Josh here. Therefore, I'm going to deal with him the way I've dealt with every other virgin who's been dropped in my lap over the last few millennia. I'm going to send him on his merry, unmolested way.

I grab my keys off the desk. A hot hand closes around my wrist. I spin around. Josh is in front of me. His cheeks are flushed, and his chest rises and falls as though he's just in from a jog on an autumn morning. Behind him, the windmill is tilted again. The keys fall from my fingers and land on the carpet with a soft thud. Delicate knuckles fold around mine.

"Please, don't do that," I whisper.

"Gideon."

It's my intention to step back, to pull my hand from his.

"You think I haven't noticed the way you're looking at me?" he says, gripping my hand tighter.

"Why are you doing this?"

"I don't know." He licks his lower lip. "But, I'm supposed to be here, Gideon. I think we both feel that."

I stand perfectly still. Josh interprets my silence as consent. His face moves close to mine and he smells so damn gorgeous. I want to lick him all over. At the last minute, I press my lips to his jaw and slide them up to his ear.

"Bad idea," I say.

He drops his face into the hollow of my shoulder. My palms rumble down his spine. I rub my cheek over his hair. The lingering scent of clean sweat and fear mingles with apples and sudden arousal.

Our lips meet in a chaste introduction. But when his tongue slips across the border, I suck it back, trapping it against the roof of my mouth. For the first time, I taste what I've craved for thousands of years. My tongue dips into the dark space under his, and I can almost hear the ecstatic cramp of his salivary glands as liquid heat purls into that secret reservoir. I shouldn't be kissing Josh at all, let alone drinking of him. A low moan travels up his throat and down mine. Our mouths melt together like hot wax and honey.

I nearly fall backward when he presses the length of his slight body against me. My hard-on prods at his stomach. I wrench my mouth away. Josh clings to me, his lips and teeth fastening on my neck in that clumsy teenage fashion that leads to hickeys and other visible wounds. I run my hands under his shirt, over his back and shoulders. Wiry muscles twitch beneath skin soft and smooth as any girl's.

Josh crushes his pelvis against my thigh. He's hard, so hard. A line of saliva falls from my lips at the thought of tasting that hardness – licking him, sucking him, making him come, and letting him run down my throat. I want to force myself into his virgin body and pump into him hard and fast like a galloping heart, gone toxic with adrenaline. Those hazel eyes will weep as pleasure bleeds into pain. Ecstasy riven by a keen edge.

I clench my jaw. I've been fighting so long and I'm so *hungry*.

"Gideon. I want you." I stifle a tormented growl when he tentatively strokes me through my jeans. "Please," he says. "I want you to be my first. I need it to be you."

I grab his wrist. "You really don't."

"Then just touch me. Let me touch you."

There's an idea. Just touching. It's the thinnest of red lines, but perhaps as long as neither of our dicks get stuck somewhere they don't belong...

I push him against the wall between the front door and the windmill, unbutton his jeans and draw down the zipper with a muffled whirr. I grip him through his shorts, too hard. He winces, but doesn't tell me to stop. Thank God. If he were to say no at this point, his fate would be sealed.

He buries his face in my shoulder. I jerk him off through his underwear, because I don't trust myself with skin-to-skin contact. Moisture seeps through and his breathing turns to a harsh pant. I can't help it. I withdraw my hand.

"Fuck." Josh stiffens, his voice hoarse. "Don't stop. Please."

"Shh…" My fingertips skate between jutting hipbones and dive below the elastic. Josh utters a starving sob. Fingers dig hard into my shoulders. I'm just short of rough with him.

He starts to tremble. "Jesus. Gideon!"

Two names that should never keep parallel company – Josh is plainly unaware of this as he spills hot over my knuckles and the staggered thump of his heart against my chest pushes me to the brink. I force myself to step back, allowing him to retain both technical virginity and a pulse. My hand itches. I fight the urge to lick. Instead, I yank some tissues from the box on my desk.

Josh flushes further as he tucks himself back into his pants and rakes a hand through his tousled hair. He looks up at me with his almost-smile. My empty arms ache, and he steps into them easily, like it's the only place he's ever belonged. I tuck him against my body, wanting to protect him, to make him feel safe. When did I last hold someone like this? When did someone last hold me?

"I'm not sure what to do," he says. His eyes drop away from mine and he shifts his weight from foot-to-foot, like the awkward teenager he is.

I cup his face in my hands. *Amour, Ammaru, dragoste, sayang, armastas, szeretet.* I'm the oldest thing on the planet and I can say the word in every language ever spoken. But I've never *felt* it, not like this. I'm not confused either – an impatient hand job barely qualifies as sex, let alone love. I didn't even come.

My lips move against his. "You need to go."

Josh explodes out of my arms, nearly tripping over the coffee table. "What's that supposed to mean?"

"It means, this is wrong." I move to steady him, but he jerks back. "You shouldn't be giving it away to a stranger just because it's convenient."

"You think this is about convenience?" he says. "I'm a virgin by choice, Gideon. If I wanted to give it away, I would have done it a long time ago."

He jams his hands in his pockets. Angry. He's beautiful

and I want him. I want more from him than he'd be willing to give.

He moves closer. "Gideon. I want this. I want you."

"You don't know what you're saying." I cross the room, putting the coffee table between us. "You've been kidnapped, and I'm the world's biggest creep. I'm going to take you home, where you can eat French toast with your mom and dad and forget this whole thing ever happened."

"You don't know anything about me." Josh sidesteps the table to poke his finger into my chest. "I don't like French toast, and my mom is a total wackadoo, who, to this day, won't tell me who my father is, so the closest thing I have to a dad is my Grandpa Dave. And anyway, I don't live with them."

"Where the hell do you live, then?"

"Few years ago I moved in with my friend, Maggie." He flops down on the sofa and squeezes a silk throw pillow to his chest. "She always thought Jared was an asshole. She knew. But I didn't listen to her."

I join him on the sofa, but leave the middle cushion as a buffer. "I know how it feels when people you care about change, turn bad."

"He outed me for thirty minutes of popularity. He called me a fag and then he laughed this mean, squinty-eyed laugh. Like the whole time we were friends, he was only pretending. That he hated me." The heel of his hand swipes at his eyes. Then that hand, damp with Honeycrisp tears, squeezes mine. "You don't know me, Gideon. But I know you. I know you're scared. There's a reason I'm here. It's the same reason you're trying to shove me out of your life like a leper."

I can't help smiling. "And what would you do if a leper showed up at your door?"

"Guess I'd try to help him, if I could."

"You've never seen leprosy up close."

I want to know more about him. He obliges, describing his mom as a Mormon convert whose sporadically-medicated schizophrenia drove him to move in with Maggie when he was in the eleventh grade, and Maggie was still turning tricks to pay the rent. He meets with Grandpa Dave every Sunday for cheese Danishes and coffee. Maggie sometimes joins them. His mother, whom Josh refers to as Moira, hasn't spoken to him in over a year.

"She thinks having me ruined her life," he says. "And it makes me feel like shit, but she's still my mom, you know? There's a lot I want to tell her before…but she won't talk to me."

He takes a moment, then parks that story and moves on to tell me about how the day after graduation, he hit the road and lived for two months alone in the wilderness of Northern Alberta. I ask him why.

"To figure out who I am when no one else is around," he says, as though it should be obvious.

What's obvious is that, at nineteen, Josh is more self-aware than most middle-aged men. He explains that when he returned from his walkabout, he got a haircut, cancelled his enrollment at the university, and decided to work full-time with the kids.

I've migrated onto the middle cushion. "Why don't you want to go to school, Josh?"

"No." His hand moves to my thigh. "You've been interrogating me for the last hour. What's your deal? You don't really want me to leave."

My skin tingles under his touch, but I'm detached from the sensation. I feel far away from myself, and yet, so close to Josh. I could pass right through his skin and live behind his eyes. What would it be like to float in the consciousness of someone so forgiving?

His hand lifts mine and his eyes fall shut, dark lashes casting shadows over his cheeks. His lips brush the inside of my wrist. My radial artery hammers against his mouth. When his strange eyes open, they hold me in traction. I know those eyes. And He knows me.

I struggle to my feet and press my knuckles into my teeth. I can't breathe. Rage and hunger combine and expand like noxious foam, and take up too much space, and crowd against my secrets, and it isn't possible, and I can't breathe.

"Who are you?" I gasp. Josh leaps up and rests his hand lightly on my arm. I jerk away. "Tell me the truth, Joshua Lamb. What did He promise you? What are you expecting from a God who would sacrifice you so cheaply?"

Josh backs away. "Gideon, you're scaring me."

"Good! Because I'm not the person you think I am. I'm not a person at all."

His heart pounds and I don't want to hear it. I don't want to know that the curving white bars of a flimsy cage are all that separates me from what I'm dying to sink my teeth into. As his blood pressure rises, I can see his external jugular press against the skin of his neck. My eyes linger on the bifurcation where those venous tributaries converge. Salvation and damnation pour into a single path leading straight to the heart.

I drop to the carpet in front of the couch and wrap my arms around my drawn up knees. Holding myself together. I hear Josh move around behind me. I wait for the front door to slam. Instead, he kneels beside me on the floor.

His arms slide around my shoulders. "Gideon, you can trust me."

And I do, though I should know better. The last time I looked into the eyes of someone who knew me, the last time I dared to hope... I press my forehead to his. Sweet breath washes over my face and his fingers trail through my hair. My father said he fell in love with Lilith the moment he landed on her shoulder. I never fully believed him, until now.

"Tell me who you are," he says. A gentle command.

I start at the beginning and leave out nothing. His expression remains neutral as I confess the atrocities committed by my family, and the ravenous beast perpetually gnawing at my self-control. Then, I tell him about my attempts to be good. Building orphanages in Cambodia, irrigation ditches in Zimbabwe, interpreting for the Red Cross in war zones. All the things I did until I couldn't be around people anymore.

"And it's not enough. It can never be enough." I bury my face in my hands. "I want it to stop. But there's only one way it can end."

Something flares in Josh's eyes. He's too young to understand how someone could want to die, especially knowing they'd go straight to *helvete*. He doesn't understand that I'm already there.

"You don't want to hurt anyone," he says carefully. "But, you will."

I look away, as if it can insulate me from the truth. "I have to try. I don't have a choice."

"You do now," Josh says. "Take me."

I scuttle backward across the carpet and clamber to my feet, my ears ringing.

"Just listen, okay?" He remains cross-legged on the floor. "Since the Flood, you've been doing all this good stuff, trying to make it right. But you're the last, Gideon. Your work is done and you're not as bad as you think you are. You deserve to go home, to be with your family again. I want to help you."

"Are you out of your mind?"

"I'm dying."

"What?" I grope blindly for support and find the rounded corner of the desk.

"Hypertrophic cardiomyopathy. I've got another year. Maybe." He worries his lower lip for just a moment before resolve sets in. "I want to give you my heart, Gideon. While I still can, while it's still beating."

All I hear is the soft tick of the clock on the desk behind me. I want him to take it back, but I know he won't. He's made his peace. It's surreal. I woke up to an ordinary Monday with an inconvenient package on my front porch. Now, this could be my last day on Earth. Our last day.

The clock ticks and my feet whisper across the carpet. I sink to my knees and pull him, warm and alive, into my arms. "You don't know who you are, do you?"

"Maybe not," he says, his cheek hot against mine. "Or, maybe I know more than you think. Does it matter?"

"You don't deserve to die like this."

"I don't deserve to die at all. Doesn't change the fact that it's coming up on checkout time for me. That's not my choice. But you are."

I hold him tighter. "I can't."

"Do you think this is a coincidence?" He rises to his feet. "This is why I'm here, Gideon. To help you."

His words heave up a poorly digested memory. When I first heard them, I was hopeful, grateful. Now I'm horrified. I would never ask this of him. I can still say no.

Josh retrieves the knife from under the newspaper and notes my surprise. "What, you thought I didn't see this?"

Without any hesitating hash marks, he slices the inside of his chafed wrist. Blood beads and runs. My stomach clenches.

"Take it." He offers his bleeding wrist.

I shake my head and dig my fingers into the carpet until my knuckles crack. Josh shrugs and drags the blade over his other wrist, a little deeper this time. Deep, but not fatal. Blood patters onto the floor. The knife falls and he holds his hands out, palms up.

"Goddammit, Gideon." He scowls and kneels in front of me, hands on either side of my neck, his blood running onto my chest. "You're the only person I've ever wanted this way. I want your mouth on me. I want your cock inside me. I want you to drink my blood and eat my heart – it's no good to me, anyway – and when it's over, we'll both be free."

It's as logical a suicide pact as I've ever heard.

I reach for his wrist. An unstoppable chain reaction is ignited the second my lips touch his skin. Blood runs poison-apple red down my throat, teasing me with the taste of raw flesh as I tongue the wound. I moan in carnal anticipation of everything I've ever wanted, but couldn't let myself imagine. There's a grinding ache too, knowing Josh is giving it freely. For that, I owe him something. I'll be as gentle as I can, for as long as I can. But, at some point, the monster will surface.

I dive for his other bleeding wrist. Our eyes lock as I seal my mouth around the gash, pulling another red mouthful from his open veins. He watches with an expression of shock and something else that tells me the experience isn't entirely unpleasant for him.

I drink and drink. Here, in the moment, but also outside myself again. I think of the draining sink. Water, coffee and soapsuds. Where does it all go? We think – we believe – it gets piped into the septic tank or pulled back to a treatment plant. Reclaimed. But, does it really? There's a question of faith. Clockwise drainage in the northern hemisphere, counter-clockwise in the south. Gravity or the Earth's rotation or something. Myth. It's the shape of pipes, that's all. There's no overriding force, but inevitability. In the end, we all get fed to the drain.

The bleeding has almost stopped. I tear his shirt over his head, revealing smooth, butterscotch skin. My shirt follows, landing on the tiles of the hearth. He kisses me, hard, and a groan rumbles out of his chest. I know it's the blood. Does it taste the same to him? Like Honeycrisp apples? We stand up and kick off the rest of our clothes. Naked, we're different as can be. A giant – pale, muscular and immortal. A teenager – dark and willowy, with a bad heart. Josh gives me a shy, but appreciative, once-over that makes me want to kiss the corners of his mouth and lick the skin behind his knees.

Then, it hits me: I'm still in control. Yes, I want to do terrible things to him, but I'm not turning into a monster. Not yet.

I take him down to the blood-speckled carpet. A fresh stream from his slashed wrist begs my attention. His stomach muscles contract under my lips and unshaven cheeks. He cries out and arches his back as I do things with my fingers and tongue that he's never felt before and never will again. God help me, but that knowledge only makes it hotter.

Twining his fists in my hair, he drags me back up to his mouth, whispering, "Fuck me."

The monster cracks open one yellow eye and its claws spring free. I stare down into his face. He's calm, but I can see the fear, and I hate myself.

"Josh, I love you. And not just for doing this."

He gives me his almost smile, the one that dimples his cheek. "I know."

"I'm sorry," I say and kiss him one last time. My final act of kindness.

His initial gasp of pain is too much. I snap like an over-tuned piano wire and thrust hard. He bucks beneath me and I feel him bite down on a scream, but I can't stop. Eventually, he starts moving with me. I gather him close and feel his invisibly flagging heart crash against my sternum. I can see it in my mind. Wet. Hot. Throbbing with life-giving purpose.

"Gideon," he whispers and comes over his stomach.

I'm still moving inside him when steel gleams in my

periphery. My mouth floods. The monster roars. I grasp the wooden handle. The blade catches a flash of morning light, streaming through the leaves of the Rowan tree. A brief reflection of a swallow taking flight. I cry out and plunge the knife into his chest.

Josh's mouth opens in breathless shock. Tears roll down his temples. I orgasm, and the ecstatic grief devours me from the inside. The blade pulls free with a sucking sound. His face is ash grey. His body trembles. The blood shivers.

Now, I am the monster, and the monster is me. My breath grates like a hacksaw through dry spruce. Life is running out. Must act quickly. His ragged scream sings in my ears when I dig my fingers into the wound. With one great burst of Nephilim strength, I crack his sugar-white ribs open and expose the jewel beneath.

Red and glistening, raw and meaty, it pulses in spite of the purple-black slash nearly cutting it in two. And the smell – apples laced with iron. Josh's blue lips move. No sound comes out, but I hear him.

I love you, Gideon. Finish it.

I plunge my hands into his open chest and rip his traitor heart from its moorings. The gelatinous snap and tear is nauseating, even as my stomach growls. His face contorts in agony and his spine bows in a taut arch. It's beautiful. He's beautiful.

Blood rains down my arms as I bring the quivering organ to my mouth. Setting my teeth into the hot, rubbery muscle, I crank my jaw shut. The gush of live flesh torn apart drenches my throat with a fresh tide of blood that surpasses everything I thought I knew about pleasure.

I look down at his face. Chalky skin, hazel eyes turned upward, vacant. His heart rests heavy and unmoving in my hands. He's gone. Tears spill over and cut tracks through the gore on my face.

Forgive me.

I tenderly place the remains of his heart back into his mangled chest cavity. With a bloody hand, I close his eyelids and kiss them. I kiss his mouth, his forehead, his hands.

Forgive me. Forgive me…

I repeat my silent mantra in every language I know, until I feel a draft. I look up into large brown eyes, regarding me, not with disgust, but compassion. A silver sword rests in his hand.

"Gabriel," I croak.

"Weep not Gideon, son of Lucifer. You are forgiven."

I shake my head. "Why?"

"All that you seek, you will find on the other side of the veil."

Gabriel raises his sword and draws a thread of fire across my throat. Blood fans across Josh's ruined corpse. My elbows buckle. Gideon's body becomes Joshua's shroud. I circle the drain, perhaps clockwise. With a gentle hand on Josh's forehead, Gabriel murmurs a low benediction, resolving an ancient curse with a final, forbidden Word.

Then, Gabriel is gone. The Word lingers.

"Jehovah," I whisper, delivered from bondage through the last labor of an immortal heart. Beating. Still.

~

Why(Y)
~

We don't need to say it. Some things you just know, because you feel them, deep in your chest, in the quiet space behind your heart.

When you come in this time, you're almost smiling. Maybe not for me. I smile back anyway. You're different, as always, but I know what to look for. There's a violence about you, a disarrangement of the underneath. The 'Y' tells the story. I know what they did. They opened you up, investigated your insides. Why? To determine how, of course. That which lived in darkness, dragged dead into the light. Weighed and measured. Dissected and curated. Stuffed back in and zipped back up. When I think of what you've been through...and still you smile, almost.

You wait while I file paperwork and tuck the others in for the night. I try not to rush, that's how mistakes get made, but it's been months and I ache with missing you, like my insides are all backwards and out of order. Still, I'm glad we have a few minutes to catch up before it's time to go. I do the talking. That's how well I know you. I don't just finish your sentences; I start them, too. There was a time – so long ago I hardly remember it – when you would speak and sing, and mouth the words of a book as you read them. Your mouth is closed now, but you're here. And it's enough.

I wheel you into the garage. Are you self-conscious about your handicap? Surely, you must know I don't think of you any differently. In the car, you need your rest, so I leave you in peace as I drive us home. From one garage, into another.

Straight to bed we go. I adjust the pillow under your head until you look comfortable. No matter how cold you are, you'll never ask for another blanket. Good thing I always know what you need. I open the chest at the foot of the bed and pull out a quilt. It's blue, like a patch of sunny sky. You love the sun, though your skin won't tolerate it for long. We learned that the hard way, didn't we? Better to live in the dark than to die in the light.

The quilt helps, but there's no substitute for body heat. I undress and slide under the covers next to you. The fit isn't jigsaw puzzle perfect, but as I wedge myself under your arm and lay with my front pressed to your side, I find my head settles nicely in the hollow beneath your shoulder.

I do miss you. I hate that I'm so needy, that I can't help what I want. Not much, just skin. That's all. Is that so wrong? I want to be close to you. As close as I can get before you leave me again. I know you'll come back – you'll be different, though. Sometimes better, sometimes worse. Looks aren't everything, but certain faces are harder. Sometimes my eyes hardly recognize you. Thankfully, the dark space behind my heart always knows.

This time, your face is easy and your body is beautiful. Young, smooth muscles. Skin, pale and hairless. A rare treat. I suck in my stomach and hook my leg over yours.

With my eyes and fingers, I learn the new you. Exploration and cartography. Science, but also ritual. I catalogue all your shapes and colors and bumps and dips. Finally I come to those familiar, bloodless wounds, the ones you always carry, no matter how your face changes. Why(Y)? Why is it never enough? My hands travel slow and quiet. Not so cold anymore. I wish you'd be more aggressive. Just once, I wish *you* would kiss *me*. It's all right. I understand your limitations.

A weary weight sinks into my bones, but we have to make the most of this time. They'll be expecting you tomorrow. People coming to say 'goodbye' and 'see you later'.

For now, it's only us. You're warmer, now. It's my warmth, finding you the way you always find me.

Don't worry about a thing. Don't I always take care of you? I'll make sure you're ready. On time, dressed in your best, and more or less whole. No need to introduce me to your family, or your friends. Better for them to look through me. I'll watch you go, and I'll wait for you to come back. I'll look for the incision, the Why(Y) carved in flesh.

Rest now. Lie with me. You don't need to say a word.

~

Three Minutes

~

Wake up, wake up, wake up…

John's breath scraped his throat and his hands ached from the sheets twisted tight around his fingers. His silent chant looped through the dark.

The Dream Eater was close. It bashed the gates of the real world and clawed at him through the bars. In a fading whisper, it told secrets he didn't want to know, in words he couldn't understand.

Every night, for as long as he could remember, the Dream Eater chased him through the black nothing of sleep. He'd done the math, and had since then kept track. At twelve years, seven months and three days old that was 4599 nights of jolting awake with his heart trying to crack through his chest like an alien baby.

Tonight made it an even 4600.

Sweat pooled in his ears as he stared at the ceiling and listened to the roar of the fan, churning thick summer air. By the time his heart relaxed, he wasn't sure what made it spaz out in the first place. The memory was gone. It dissolved that way every night, leaving him with a skull crammed full of bad feelings he couldn't explain.

It was after midnight, but the room still baked with the heat of the day. The four boys he bunked with were motionless lumps in their beds. John was wide-awake. He sucked at sleeping. It was called insomnia. He had a book

81

about it hidden under his mattress. The book said chronic insomnia was rare in children. The book also said kids who couldn't sleep were usually messed up. John figured foster care was enough to warp anyone's brainpan. But it was all he'd ever known.

A shaft of light from a streetlamp fell across the crucifix on the wall beside his bed. John didn't believe in God, but felt sort of bad for plastic Jesus, melting on His cross.

Hot as hell, John thought. Then he turned his face into the pillow and laughed. It *was* hot as hell. He'd long since kicked away the covers, and his pajama pants clung to his skinny legs like wet towels. Even in the dark he could see the dinosaur pattern.

Too freaking babyish to believe.

It sucked to be a shrimp when you were stuck with what fit from the hand-me-down heap. He flipped his pillow and sighed as the cool surface cradled his head.

The fan growled.

Sleep? Yeah, right. Waste of time, anyway. While the world snored, he could do whatever he wanted. And there were better things to do than lay in the dark and sweat. He rolled out of bed, ditched the dino-pants, and pulled on a t-shirt, cut-off jeans and his sneakers. Then he bundled an extra blanket under the covers. Good enough to pass an open-door bed check.

From the wall, plastic Jesus saw everything and said nothing. When John was halfway out the window, however, he heard the squeak of mattress springs.

Wendell's paper-plate face hovered in the darkness. "Where you goin'?"

"Go back to sleep."

"I'm gonna tell Monique."

John gritted his teeth.

Monique, the housemother. A holy tank of a woman who could roll over a land mine and not feel it. Monique treated

John more or less like a catastrophe in human form, like he'd personally nailed plastic Jesus to his plastic cross. Sneaking out was high on her list of Very Bad Things, and Wendell was a well-known snitch. If he tattled, it would be the kiss of death for John's nocturnal walkabouts.

Wendell was a problem.

"Tell anyone," John said, "and I'll cut your goddamn tongue out."

Wendell's paper head vanished under his blanket.

John rolled his eyes and dropped onto the lower pitch of the roof. The lattice creaked as he climbed down to the flowerbed. He was careful not to squash the plants. When you were up to Very Bad Things, it was smart not to leave evidence behind.

He brushed soil over his footprints. Then he ran. Frame houses gave way to dented trailers and empty lots full of ragweed. He held his breath as he sprinted past the latter, a runty orphan with allergies. At least he'd been spared freckles and red hair.

At the edge of town, he flew onto a path curling through a grove of aspens. His sneakers thumped on the dirt in a steady rhythm. He slowed to a panting trot when the path ended and the trees opened onto the shoreline of a man-made lake. The 'beach' was nothing more than rocks and sour mud, squishy enough to slurp the shoes off your feet. He hopped stone-to-stone until he reached the dock. There, he took a minute to catch his breath and rub the sweat from his eyes with his shirt. Starlight glinted off still black water.

He'd tried so many times, come so close. Three minutes.

He stripped to his underwear, raced down the warped planks and dove, headfirst, into warm water that tasted like bagged grass clippings after a week in the sun. When he surfaced, he took a dozen rapid breaths. It was a pearl diver trick he'd read about. Carbon dioxide was the automatic breath trigger, not oxygen. If you scrubbed most of the carbon dioxide out of your blood, you could hold your breath a lot longer.

He filled his lungs one last time. He pulled and gulped and packed the air in until it pushed his stomach out and stretched his ribs apart. Then he went under. Starlight disappeared as he flipped himself head down and kicked.

Since he didn't have a waterproof watch, he had to count in his head. One hundred eighty was the magic number. The closest he'd ever come was one hundred sixty-four. On the bottom of the lake, he pulled himself along by grabbing handfuls of slimy grass. Pulling and counting, pulling and counting. He hit eighty-three seconds when he located the cluster of man-sized rocks.

Glacial erratics – that's what they were called. Chunks of mountains chipped off and carried away by traveling glaciers during the ice age. When the ice melted, it dropped them wherever. All alone in a place they didn't belong. Odd rocks. Misfits. John knew what that was like.

One hundred twenty. Two minutes.

The need to exhale pounded at the base of his throat. Bubbles flew from his mouth as his lungs partially deflated. Like a freshwater starfish, he latched onto one of the rocks. Sharp edges, slick with algae, bit into his arms and legs. Mud squelched between his toes as they wedged in at the base.

One hundred sixty.

Almost there. His heart banged against his ribs and the numbers slopped around in his head.

One hundred seventy.

He pressed his forehead hard into the rock.

One hundred seventy-five.

Dirty air raced up his throat.

One hundred seventy-eight...nine...one hundred eighty.

Three minutes.

He braced his feet and pushed off. Instead of launching

upward, his foot sunk deep into the mud. The rock shifted onto his ankle. Not enough to crush, but enough to pin. He tugged at his leg and shoved at the rock. Panic swept his oxygen-starved brain. One thought. Three words.

Up. Air. Breathe.

Nothing worked anymore. His legs went limp and his head fell back to face the surface. Too dark. Too far. His arms flopped like they had minds of their own. Maybe the arms thought they could swim away and save themselves. But it was too late for them. Too late for everything.

His throat gasped open. For a speck of time, there was relief—until water boiled into his lungs. The reflexive cough pulled in another scalding wave. Then, like a drawstring pulled tight, his windpipe closed. His body strangled itself even as he continued to suck water into his stomach.

Air hunger, serious air hunger, was the weirdest thing. It transformed time into a melted marshmallow that stretched out forever on a single sticky thread. It also hurt more than he thought anything could. Still, he managed a few clear thoughts.

He'd read about drowning. Now he wished he hadn't. He'd rather not know about the freshwater rushing into his veins, fattening his red blood cells until they exploded, and that with each second of increasing hypoxia, his brain cells were croaking by the zillions. His throat remained sealed. It was called laryngospasm, and it wouldn't release until he passed out or went into cardiac arrest. But he didn't black out.

Instead, he felt the last link between his mind and its meat-suit, snap. Then he felt nothing at all.

Interesting.

Death was a dark, floaty place, like the bottom of the lake, except he didn't have to hold his breath, because he had no body that needed to breathe. If there was a white light, he had no eyes to see it, and no legs to walk toward or away from it. As he floundered, it occurred to him that his last words were, *"I'll cut your goddamn tongue out"*. It was only meant to terrorize that snitch, Wendell, but what if there was a God? *He* probably wouldn't like that.

Monique made Hell sound like an overgrown, spider-infested garden, with each descending circle weedier than the last. Then again, what if Heaven was a giant church, with a giant bloody Jesus hanging from the wall? What if you had to sit between God and Monique on those hard benches and read the Bible forever and pretend you liked it? He'd rather spend an eternity sneezing in the weeds.

And what about reincarnation?

If that was the deal, his Karma was a problem. The foster home looked civilized on the outside, but within those walls, the law of the jungle reigned. To survive, you kept your claws sharp and used them. John was a survivor, or he had been, before he died.

No one would care much. People would think of all the Very Bad Things he'd done and say it was for the best. No one would consider that he'd done most of those bad things for good reasons.

In terms of reincarnation, he figured the best he could hope for would be an intelligent animal. Something that couldn't drown would be cool. His argument for manta ray was coming together when a voice punctured the silence. A voice he knew.

The Dream Eater.

It called his name, his *real* name. The one he had before some dud of a social worker labeled an abandoned baby 'John'. But every time the Dream Eater said the name, it would slip away before he could slot it into his memory.

"Why can't I keep it?" John asked.

"Names change, they are not important."

"Then why keep it a secret?"

"You place value on that which has none," the Dream Eater said.

"I don't believe you."

"So you have indicated, rather stridently, every night of your life. We haven't much time. Abide with me now, and I will reveal all that I am able."

"I'm not going anywhere with you."

"Even if the alternative is death?"

"Who are you?"

"I am that I am."

John had more questions, angry sorts of questions, but the Dream Eater was taking him somewhere. It pulled him. Not up or down, forward or back. It pulled him through and out. Beyond. The soft marshmallow of time stretched and twisted and folded back on itself. Seconds, years, hours, days, it was impossible to know.

The mineral smell of water tickled John's nose. He was surprised to find he had a nose again, and arms and legs, and eyes, which were closed. The moment he opened them, he was horribly dizzy.

Eyes shut. Breathe deep. Try again. Eyes open. The light was wrong. An orange sun blazed in a dirty red sky. He was dressed, and dry, and standing, not by the lake, but on the bank of a river. Green water rushed fast and wide through a valley of dead trees and yellow earth.

John was alone on his side, but across the water, there were people. They were dirty, with blood on their hands and faces. A woman stumbled out of the crowd. She stood at the edge of the river, clutching a filthy towel to her chest.

Not a towel, a baby.

Her eyes met John's. She jumped into the river. He held a breath for them, but they never surfaced.

The others screamed.

They called his name. They cursed him and begged for help in a language he didn't know but somehow understood because their words were a noose around his neck, tugging him forward, until his toes hung off the edge of the steep bank. Gravity teased him closer and closer to a tumble into the rapids. Then a hand closed on his shoulder.

"Your part in saving them is long done," said a soft voice, and the hand pulled him back from the edge. In his ungentle life, it was the kindest touch John had ever felt The hand belonged to a man or someone man-shaped, but not a man at all. He had gold skin and eyes with no whites. They glowed, like the sun glinting off shards of blue glass.

"Am I dead?"

The man-that-was-not-a-man sighed and shook his head. "You weary me, stubborn thing."

"Sorry," John said, and meant it, though the very word felt strange in his mouth, and he couldn't ever remember saying it sincerely.

The man shrugged. "Faith is a fool's virtue."

John didn't know what that meant.

"You think me disingenuous."

He didn't know what that meant, either.

"But I kept only what you were not prepared to see. Look around."

John scanned the valley. No birds, no bugs, only a bone yard of barren trees and baked dirt. He listened to the heavy rush of the river and the cries of the people on the other side. "These are my dreams?"

"You are strong enough now to be shown what is true." The man gestured to the wailing mob. "Wretches. Like human names, human life is worthless. Their souls, on the other hand, are pearls of great price."

"What does this have to do with me?"

"To be saved, they must suffer." The man's blue gaze swung away from the mob. "But nature seeks a balance, and its laws are not easily subverted. I designed it to be so. As such my power here is limited. On the mortal plane, I must work through men."

John's heart fought for space between lungs that felt bloated and stiff. For 4600 nights, he thought he'd been running from a monster, or a demon. He crumpled to his knees on the cracked earth.

Balance? What the hell? I had to drown for this? A bitter taste crawled into his mouth. He spit in the dirt.

"Why don't you leave us alone?" John said. "Go burn some ants with a magnifying glass or something."

"What I speak of is no triviality. The balance must be maintained."

Balance this, was on the tip of John's tongue. "What are you talking about?"

"I made this world," He said. "It must now be unmade. Dust to dust, as they say."

John's gut tumbled like a clothes dryer full of loose change.

He dropped to one knee in front of John. "In your first incarnation, you spread my word, that as I had loved them, so should they love one another. In your short life, you suffered and sacrificed yourself to save their souls. Now I call upon you again, to reap them."

John was a glacial erratic. No one knew where he'd come from. He realized this might be the only chance he'd ever get to learn more. "Who am I?"

His eyes dimmed and sadness poured off Him like frozen rain. "Names change. But always, you are my chosen."

John shivered and rubbed his eyes. The river, the mob, and the dead valley – they weren't just dreams. Very Bad Things would happen. It would start here.

John wondered if being chosen meant he had no choice.

"You desire the truth, and the truth is this–" He bowed his head. "–They will not understand this second coming, any more than the first. There will be atrocities. They will spit on your new name as they do the old. I ask too much of you, and I weep at the thought of your burden." He took John's shoulders in the same gentle grasp that saved him from the river. "I chose you with great care. But your will is your own."

John didn't know whether to laugh or faint. A powerless god was kneeling before him, asking him to choose his side of the river.

~

Water spewed from his mouth and nose. He coughed until he thought his chest might break apart. When it passed, he was shocked to find himself in the dark, sprawled near the tree line by the lake, twenty yards from where water licked the shore.

He whipped his head back and forth.

Trees. Mud. Water. Mud. Trees.

Nothing. No one.

Somehow, he'd pulled his foot free and, with a chest full of water, climbed the dock, stepped across the stones to the grass, and passed out.

Runny foam bubbled into his mouth. Words and images skipped across the surface of his mind like flat rocks. He couldn't remember. On wobbling knees he tried to stand. That wasn't happening. Instead it seemed like an awesome idea to slump to the ground, roll to his side and puke.

~

A few blocks from the house, John sagged against a chain link fence, panting. He felt heavy, like he'd swallowed an anvil. His raw, leaky lungs worked for every breath. Nothing about it felt right. Then he realized his face was six inches from a tangle of weeds and enough pollen to make his head explode.

Oh, hell, he thought. But his nose didn't so much as itch.

By the time he dragged his carcass over the windowsill, he felt almost good again. The fan still growled in the shadows of the now almost chilly bedroom. Everyone remained asleep, and no sign of Monique. Situation normal. There was just one thing he needed to set right before he crashed.

From under his quilt, he pulled out the extra blanket he'd used as a decoy. He tucked it under his arm and crossed the room to stand over a huddled form. Wendell's blond hair trailed over his forehead and his breath whistled around the thumb between his lips. He looked like a baby, innocent like that.

John wished he'd been nicer to him. Wendell was just a little kid who hadn't learned the ropes yet. Beneath their lids, his eyes flicked back and forth. It was called Rapid Eye Movement. It meant he was dreaming. What might a snitch like Wendell dream about?

On impulse, John bent and kissed Wendell's hot cheek.

Then he shook out the blanket, refolded it into a thick square, and truly hoped Wendell was having the best dream of his life.

The alarm clock said 4:09. Earlier, John held his breath for over three minutes. Permanent brain damage started after five. Wendell fought some, but John was older and stronger. He didn't know the exact reason he had to do it, only that if he didn't, Wendell would go on to be a problem for him, a big one. The hot stink of piss burned John's nose. He held the blanket down until 4:20.

Wendell was a problem, now solved.

John thought he'd feel different, maybe guilty or scared. Why, though? Nothing that easily squished could be worth much. He unfolded the blanket, spread it over the body, and yawned as he plodded to his own bed.

The only witness hung from a cross on the wall, silent as

always. John reached out and traced the crown of thorns. Suffering and sacrifice. *He* wasn't the only one.

John's throat felt tight. His stomach lurched like it was full of tumbling rocks – or loose silver. This wasn't the first time he'd done a Very Bad Thing, a dirty job.

Plastic Jesus wouldn't betray him, though. He understood. Someone had to do it.

"I'm sorry," John whispered, and meant it.

~

Little Sister, Little Brother

~

Available for immediate occupancy.
Furnished 1BR suite in the historical Leighhaven building.
Conveniently located just outside downtown.
Quiet, well maintained, with live-in management.
Email cymbria.william@leighaven.com

~

The kid had a staring problem. From behind the first floor window, her dark eyes tracked Tate as he approached the wide stoop. Tiny hands splayed against the glass, tangled hair spilling over her shoulders – Tate figured she was five, maybe six years old. Whole milk in a plastic cup with Oreo sludge at the bottom. Maybe.

Tate didn't know much about kids, though he had two nephews. Countless times he'd stood on his brother's deck, peeling the label off a Heineken, while the boys savaged each other on the lawn. Occasionally they'd return to their respective corners for a slug of cherry Kool-Aid and Brad would offer booming encouragement as he swaggered over the grill.

Doesn't get any better than this. You're missing out, little brother. What about Shelly? Her divorce is final. Think maybe she's ready to test the waters...

Do not set me up.

You're thirty-five, Tate. The business is solid. You're looking good. What are you waiting for? What about the Internet? There's that plenty of fish thing.

Sounds like a good way to get crabs.

Man your age shouldn't be alone. Have some potato salad.

No thanks.

Fuck's the matter with you, lately?

It's mayonnaise.

One good dinner won't hurt. C'mon, Val worked all day on the food, made your favorites...

Jesus.

How many matchmaking attempts had he endured? How much mayonnaise had he eaten just to be polite? How many times had he covered at the bar because someone's crotch dropping had a ballet recital, or tae kwon do, or anthrax?

But that was then and there. This was here and now. Hundreds of kilometers. A trail he'd followed into the woods, and overnight everything changed. Because it had to.

The little girl in the window slapped her palm over her mouth. Tate swore he heard giggling through the glass. He raised a hand in a hesitant wave. Were you supposed to wave at kids you didn't know? Had he just done a Creepy Thing? With a flap of dingy skirt, the kid turned and vanished into the apartment.

Above the heavy door, a sandstone arch bore the engraving 'Leighaven Est. 1901'. Tate pressed the old fashioned buzzer and watched for movement through the smoked glass panels. He buzzed again. He waited.

As Tate reached for the handle, the door swung inward. A woman stood in the entryway. Tall enough to ride the roller coaster but short enough for him to see scalp through a razor sharp part running down the middle of her head. Dark hair bracketed her pale face. Old enough to rent a car, young enough to wear red flannel without looking frumpy. Huge, dark eyes. She stood with one hand braced against the door and one behind her back, as though expecting him to foist a Book of Mormon on her.

"You must be Tate," she said.

"Are you Cymbria?"

A groove creased her forehead and her mouth stretched diagonally. "You're thin."

"Beg your pardon?" he asked, feeling the tips of his ears sizzle.

"Never mind." She twirled and started down the dim hallway, hair swishing down her back. "Come on in, Tate. Enter, if you dare."

Lager. One of those snotty craft brews in a pint glass.

The heels of her purple Mary Janes thumped on the runner as she led him past a door marked OFFICE and into a windowless stairwell.

"Hope you like exercise," she said, her voice echoing off plaster. "We don't have a..." She snapped her fingers. Once. Twice.

"Elevator?"

"Right." She aimed a finger-thumb gun at him. "Can't put one in either, on account of all the rules around preserving heritage sites."

She reminded Tate of an anime character with her snub of a nose, crooked smile and eyes taking up half her face. Not much under that flannel, but from his vantage point three stairs down, she filled out a pair of black leggings just fine.

Tate dropped his eyes to her shoes. He didn't want to be *that* neighbor. Live-in management, the ad said. Probably she ran this place with her lumberjack boyfriend. He'd wear a matching flannel and carry a wrench the size of Tate's leg over his shoulder. *You're thin...* Tate sucked in his stomach as he followed her dainty ass up the stairs.

On the third floor, she opened a door connecting to a hallway where sconces cast nominal light over the papered walls and stamped tin ceiling. She pointed to another door with a tarnished '9' over the peephole.

"I am," she said.

"Huh?"

"I'm Cymbria. Not used to introducing myself is all. Been ages since we've had a new tenant."

Tate scanned the deserted hallway. "You could hear a hair drop in here."

"Pipes make most of the noise in this place." She pointed down the corridor. "Halls are L shaped. Around that corner there's two more suites."

"Are there many kids in the building?"

"Is that a problem?"

"No," Tate said, too quickly. "I saw a little girl, in the window out front."

"That's the office."

"Oh."

Tate waited. Cymbria stared. Maybe she was a private person. The kid had the same hair and eyes. Could be her daughter.

Without breaking eye contact, Cymbria stuck her hand down the front of her shirt and pulled out a key. "You want to do it?"

The body-warm brass melted into his hand. He slid the key into the lock and opened the door to number nine.

Crown molding joined yellow walls to the ceiling and a parquet floor gleamed in the afternoon light. Pink sofa, coffee table, and corner kitchen with a few cabinets and checkered curtains drawn across the plumbing beneath the sink. Tate poked his head into the bathroom, noting the old spotless fixtures. The bedroom had a southeast-facing window. Tate imagined the sunrise pouring onto the white duvet, spread without a wrinkle over the queen size bed.

Cymbria's shoes tapped along behind him. "Mattress is new and the sheets are fresh."

Tate waded through the mellow scent of floor wax. "This is…" Scotch. Single malt. Twelve years. "It's perfect."

Cymbria clicked her heels together. "No place like home."

Tate chuckled. "Got a pen, Dorothy?"

"Oh!" She clapped her hands. "You know that book?"

"Saw the movie as a kid," Tate said, digging in his satchel. "I'll give you first, last, and a deposit right now."

"But you just got into town." Her hands curled into fists over her stomach before she forced them down and smiled, her crooked mouth almost pretty. "Need help moving in?"

"I've got a change of clothes and my laptop in the car. Once I bring those up, I am moved in." A sheepish note crept into his voice. Tate herded it away. Wasn't like he'd abandoned a flock of small children. If he wanted to drop everything and go on a vision quest that was his own goddamn business.

Cymbria's smile didn't falter, but her throat rolled as though she'd dry-swallowed an aspirin. "There's no rush, Tate. Make like a butterfly and settle. Drop the cheques by the office tomorrow. I'll be around." She retrieved another key from her shirt and before Tate could ask how many she had in there, she'd dropped the hot brass into his hand.

"That's for the front door."

"Okay?" He trailed her as she all but fled the apartment.

"Welcome to the building!" She tossed another bent smile over her shoulder and the spring-hinged stairwell door shut behind her.

"No place like home," Tate muttered.

He sprawled on the sofa, enjoying the silence, getting to know the smell and the light. When the sun began to sink he decided to grab his bag from the car. Just as he opened the apartment door a child's laugh rang out, clear and silver.

97

Tate stepped into the hall. "Hello?"

Pattering footsteps. Tate wandered down and peered around the corner. Another hall with a window at the end, creating the illusion of being in a tunnel, or a mineshaft.

Two doors, one on either side. Tate glanced back at the sunlight slashing through the open door of his own apartment. Three units to a floor then. That made for nine suites total. Number nine. The highest room in the tallest tower. The cherry in the Shirley Temple ordered by the vocally sober or tacitly pregnant.

The floor creaked as Tate approached the window. Not a bad view. Streets lined with poplars, and the downtown skyline beyond. Tate liked the idea of living in an old building in a strange city. So long as that kid wasn't running the halls at all hours. He turned from the window and when he rounded the corner, he found himself in the dark. The wall sconces had gone out, and the door to number nine was closed.

~

Eighty-one squares on the ceiling, each stamped with concentric circles, like ripples in a puddle. Nine rows of nine. Tate lay on his back in the white bed and counted the moonlit squares again. He waited for sleep.

"What the hell am I doing?"

A reply came in the form of muffled groans and pops. The shuddering language of an old building tucking itself in for the night. Yesterday, Tate had responsibilities. He had roots. Now, he was alone in a strange bed in a strange place. No one demanding. No one needing. It didn't feel good yet, but he expected that to change soon.

Yesterday, he'd been at the bar, pouring and bussing on his own because surprise, surprise, Brad and Shelly both had family hurricanes blow in on the same night, which happened to be Thursday. The worst night in the industry.

The shift started out okay. Tate traded syllables with the math teacher who shambled in every day at four to down a variable number of rum and cokes. Bacardi dark, no lime. He'd paid his tab, left his customary five-dollar tip and shambled out. Tate had an hour of quiet before Thursday People descended. Customers looking to start the weekend early, but with the responsible adult stick still wedged far enough up their rears to ask about gluten-free menu options.

After that it was loosened ties, and high-heeled shoes dangling from painted toes. Embryonic infidelities. Cab sav and chard for the ladies, beer on tap for the gents, and a steady flow of gin and tonic filling gaps in the gender binary. Open tabs paid on plastic. Lime juice under his fingernails.

Just after ten, some hipster sashayed through the door with his scarf-twirling entourage. Eyes glued to his phone, he typed one-thumbed while snapping his fingers in the general direction of the bar. He ordered a round of sidecars.

Fucking *sidecars*.

Tate threw his rag down and walked out.

On everything.

He'd meant to go outside for a few minutes, get some air. But then he'd dipped a hand into his pocket and felt his car keys.

A few hours later, he stopped for gas. He threw his phone in the squeegee bucket. Sploosh. Gone. He didn't know why, didn't have an answer. Why? Why what? He didn't even know the question.

He just knew.

That life was done. It didn't exist anymore. He'd followed that broken line on the highway to a creaking pile smelling of damp wood and dust. Leighaven was creepy as hell, and the second he crossed the threshold, Tate knew he'd come home.

~

Tate knocked on the office door. When no one answered, he twisted the knob and poked his head in. "Hello?"

The suite was laid out like his but instead of a couch and TV, there was a desk with a printer, monitor, penholder, and a stack of unopened mail. Bookshelves stuffed with hundreds of paperbacks lined the far wall. The bedroom door was closed.

"Lost?"

Tate spun around, nearly bumping noses with the man standing behind him. Hair the color of black coffee fell over large eyes set in a pale, angular face. Taller, broader, but the resemblance was unmistakable.

"Sorry, you startled me," said Tate.

"Yeah, well." The man shoved past Tate, setting his toolbox on he desk. He dropped into the chair and reached into a basket on the floor. A pair of knitting needles emerged, trailing a mass of yellow yarn. He began casting stitches on the empty needle, hands working at a tempo you could set a metronome by. After a dozen beats, he glanced up at Tate. "What do you want?"

"Just dropping something off. For Cymbria?"

The needles clicked. "You're not sure?"

"Pardon?"

"You said it like a question." The man glowered through the hair hanging in his eyes.

"Rent, and deposit." Tate pinched the cheques between his thumb and forefinger. "I'm the new tenant in number nine."

"Right. Number nine. Here to breathe some life into the place." The man pushed his sleeves up his slender forearms and extended a hand, but not to shake. "Give 'em to me. I'll take care of it."

Tate laid the cheques across the man's palm. "Wasn't sure who to make them out to. Figured you might have a stamp or something."

"Tate Sutton," the man read off the cheque. "What the hell kind of name is that? Tate?"

Tate gritted his teeth. "And, you are?"

A smirking version of Cymbria's smile stretched across the man's face as he flipped his hair out of his eyes. "I'm Will. And I'm the fixit around here, so if you got needs, lemme know."

Jäger. That would be Tate's first guess, except tall dark and sullen here didn't have the requisite neck tattoo. So, not Jäger, but something that made a statement. People like Will took up knitting for a reason. Otherwise, they'd be serial stranglers.

"I'll tell Little Sister you stopped by."

Tate headed for the door. "Good to meet you, Will."

"Welcome to Leighaven, Tater Tot. Enjoy our stairs."

The clicking of needles started up again as Tate closed the door behind him with more force than necessary. Blood pulsed hot in his ears. *Tater Tot*. Dick. There was no way Cymbria's brother could possibly...

Screwdriver. That was it.

Perfect for Leighaven's crafty maintenance man. Nothing said, *I'm an alcoholic and I don't even care that you know,* like bottom shelf vodka with a splash of O.J. for breakfast. The get-it-done cocktail. That was Will.

In the stairwell, water stuttered through the pipes running up the walls like painted snakes. Lights blazed, but Tate froze as a sense of darkness engulfed him. Surly brothers and grouchy plumbing aside, there was a sickness about Leighaven. Something chronic and crippling. He ought to run upstairs, pack his shit, and get the hell out. Or not. He had his wallet and keys in his pocket. He didn't need anything else.

He ought to leave. Right now.

He tipped his head back, squinted at the ceiling three floors above, and knew he wasn't going anywhere.

~

Vanishing without a trace held a certain romantic appeal, but the last thing Tate wanted was to be reported as a missing person. The proof of life email he'd sent his second day at Leighaven wouldn't hold them forever. Tate stared at the pre-paid cell phone in his hand and dialed.

Brad picked up on the second ring. "Hullo?"

"Hey."

"Jesus Christ," Brad shouted into the phone.

"Thought I'd check in. It's been a few weeks."

"It's been a month and a half! What the hell? What happened? Where are you?"

"Doesn't matter. Just wanted you to know I'm okay."

"Well that's real nice, Tate. Except Val's worried sick, the boys ask about you every day, I've been tearing my hair out trying to run the bar by myself."

Tate envisioned his brother's scrunched up forehead. "I know you're pissed. I don't blame you."

"What the fuck is going on?" Brad breathed heavily into the phone. "Are you in trouble? Is it drugs? Did you get a girl pregnant?"

Tate chuckled. "No, Brad. Nothing like that."

"You're really okay?"

"I really am."

"Need money?"

"I've got money."

Between his savings and a part-time gig shelving books at the downtown library, he had enough to live on and plenty of time for reading, jogging, exploring, and lately, writing. Thirty-five years of keeping his mouth shut had left him with a surprising lot to say. But not to Brad.

"How are the boys? I miss them," Tate said, aware that it wasn't entirely true, but it seemed like the thing to say. Two minutes of conversation with his brother, and already, Tate was falling back on old habits.

"If you miss those boys, man up and tell 'em yourself," Brad gruffed and then sighed again. "This isn't like you, Tate."

"People change, Brad. Sometimes they have to."

"Look, I'm not even pissed, not really. But I trusted you to have my back, brother. You've let me down, you've let us all down..."

Commencement of the, 'I'm not angry just disappointed', speech had Tate appreciating Will's brand of open hostility. He wished Brad would just give him hell. Then Tate could shovel it right back. Point out that it was easy to feel let down when you weren't used to hauling your own goddamn weight. Remind Brad that until six weeks ago Tate always had his back. Always. But in the three decades prior, when exactly did Brad ever have his? Fat Tate never had anyone behind him. Because Fat Tate was the omega. Always.

"A man works hard and takes care of his family..."

Christ almighty... Tate pinched the bridge of his nose.

"Now, that means something to me, and it used to mean something to you..."

He had clothes in the dryer downstairs. They'd be done about now. Brad went on scolding. Tate shoved the phone between the pink sofa cushions and walked out, shutting the door to number nine behind him.

A blur whipped around the corner of the hallway. Shadows had a way of coming to life at Leighaven. Things moved. Loud cracks and what sounded uncannily like wordless shouting erupted at all hours, keeping him on his toes. Tate felt awake here. Present and engaged in a way he'd never before experienced.

Fluorescent tubes buzzed on the basement ceiling, illuminating windowless cinder brick walls, painted an institutional green. Just a laundry room. Not like it had to be airy and tastefully appointed. Still, something a little less cryptacular would be nice. He'd only ever had reason to enter the laundry room but if he did take a stroll around the bend in the corridor, he'd be disappointed not to find a pair of skeletons tossing bourbon down their fleshless gullets and telling each other knock-knock jokes.

A rivet on a pair of jeans branded Tate's arm as he pulled his clothes out of the dryer. He wondered if Brad was still hectoring the recesses of the old sofa. With a smile in his heart, he picked up his full laundry basket.

The lights stopped buzzing. Tate gripped the basket handles, his palms slick on the plastic. Fluorescent tubes flickered, and died. Darkness dropped like a black bag over his head.

Tate's breath rolled in his ears. Then he became aware of another sound creeping toward him. Around him.

Pat, pat, pat.

The lights crackled on. She stood in the doorway, the ragamuffin from the window, the girl with the silver laugh. Her little chest heaved as she breathed hard but noiseless. She smiled. If smile was the right word. It might have been, if not for the drool oozing through the gaps between her teeth, running over her chin and dripping onto the concrete floor. *Pat, pat, pat.*

Tate followed the trail of viscous blobs over the floor where they led back to him. Circled him. Her ghoulish grin widened, then she turned and ran.

"Hey." Tate chased after her and stepped into the stairwell, just in time to catch a glimpse of her scuffed, yellow rain boots. Her footsteps stamped up and around, up and around, all the way to the third floor, his floor, where he heard the door open and shut.

Another face appeared over the rail at the top floor. Small face. Small boy. *So*, Tate thought, *there are two of them.*

"Stay away from her," the boy said in a pitchy snarl. He and the girl shared the same wild dark hair, and that attitude was all Will. There had to be some relation.

"Lights went out," Tate said. "I didn't mean to scare her."

"Scared? Of you?" The little boy scoffed and turned away from the rail. Tate heard the door open and snap shut again.

"Brats," Tate muttered.

When he reached the third floor, he heard no laughter, or disembodied footsteps. No sign of the kids. They had to live in one of the other two units on his floor. Tate unlocked number nine, stepped onto the sunny parquet floor, and left all consternation behind. He was glad he'd blocked the number to the burner phone and deactivated his email account. It was nice to come home and not dread sorting through messages. It was nice to come home.

~

The office door was ajar, nevertheless he knocked.

"Hi Tate, come on in."

He walked in to find Cymbria sitting cross-legged on the desk, dipping a graham cracker into a can of frosting, eyes glued to the tablet balanced on her knee.

"How'd you know it was me?"

"Lucky guess," she said without looking up. She took a bite of the loaded cracker and sprayed crumbs as she whooped with laughter. She held up the tablet, showing him a video of a kitten wrestling with a balled up piece of paper. "Isn't it the funniest?"

Tate had opinions about the sort of people who watched cat videos. But it was hard not to smile at a kitten being a kitten. Just like it was hard not to laugh at Cymbria's latest wackadoodle get up. Denim cut-offs over orange tights and pink Converse sneakers. She also wore a slouchy yellow sweater. A sweater Tate had last seen several weeks ago on her brother's knitting needles.

Little Big Bird's eyes slid over him as she stretched out her endless orange legs.

"Want some?"

"Pardon?"

She held out a graham cracker and the can of frosting. "It's the best snack I ever invented."

Tate shook his head. "Sounds great, but it's not for me."

"Y'know, people with nothing to lose usually come to a bad end. Think about that before you give up everything good in life."

She looked so utterly serious, and Tate couldn't help himself. He swiped a dot of icing from the corner of her mouth with his thumb, and licked it clean. "I haven't given up *everything* good."

"We'll see about that." She grinned and brushed crumbs off her orange tights. "So? How may I serve you today?"

Tate splashed through the brackish convergence of thoughts at the inlet of his mind, trying to locate the reason he'd popped into the office.

"There's a couple kids living here. Boy and a girl?"

Clueless eyes stared up at him.

"Do you know who they belong to?" he prompted.

Her nose wrinkled. "That's a terrible question."

"It is?"

"Who do you belong to? Who does anyone belong to?" She stuck out her confetti-hued tongue. "That's super personal. You can't just... It's a weird question. You're weird for asking it."

He was weird? Maybe she wasn't craft beer. Maybe she was something else. Like a syrupy white zin. Any self-respecting grownup would be embarrassed, but somehow, she turned it around so he was the loser, in business casual, with his glass of pinot noir.

Tate jammed his hands in his back pockets. "They run wild. Follow me around the building. I hear them outside my door. Couple days ago they were in the basement, skulking about. Someone just needs to tell them it's not cool to sneak up on strangers, and I'm not sure it should be me."

Cymbria tilted her head. "Are you strange?"

"I'd like to speak to their parents," he said. "I should probably meet my neighbors, anyway."

"Do you want to meet them?"

Tate considered it. He heard water running, footsteps, and latching doors. He received either a cheery wave from Cymbria, or a grudging nod from Will almost every day when he passed the office on his way out of the building. Otherwise, it was easy to pretend he had Leighaven all to himself.

"Guess I've been enjoying the bubble," he admitted.

A curious smile slanted across Cymbria's face. "Did you get yourself a present?"

Tate followed her pointing finger to a cardboard slab resting against the wall. "Must be the desk I ordered."

Her face fell. "That's not a present. People use desks for work."

"Or watching cat videos." Tate crouched in front of the box, inspecting the bill of lading taped to the side. "But work is the idea, yes."

Cymbria knelt beside him, her elbow not quite touching his. She gathered her hair, exposing her pale nape before tossing the dark mass over her shoulder. She smelled like kindergarten – graham crackers and hot, sticky hands. "What do you do for work, Tate?"

"Shelve books at the library."

Cymbria ran the tip of her tongue along her upper lip. "I mean before you came to Leighaven."

Not the name of the city, or even a vague 'here'. Leighaven. Like it had been his plan, all along.

"Speaking of personal questions." Tate stood up. Cymbria remained on her knees, staring up at him, her mouth soft, damp, and open just a little. He gripped the edge of the box. "Uh, I ought to get this put away, but if you want to come by later, I could pour you a cup of coffee and tell you all about it."

She blinked, a slow sweep of eyelashes. "I should get Will."

Granted it wasn't Tate's smoothest move. The kind of invitation usually met with some version of, 'Jeez, I would but I have jury duty'. It was Cymbria though, and because she had to be weird about everything, she shut him down with one unexpected syllable.

"Will?" he asked.

Cymbria bounced up and drummed her fingers on the cardboard. "To help you. Little Brother moves heavy stuff all the time. He's really strong."

Rejection, followed by three flights of hate-face?

"It's not that heavy."

It was very heavy.

"Once I get it on the first step, it'll slide up, no problem."

He said a prayer for his back.

Sweat prickled along his hairline and his shoulder ached. He focused on the door to the third floor. One more flight. He gripped the sides of the box and shoved. His toe slipped off the edge of the stair, the box slid back, hitting him in the chest. Tate's hand flew out, but his fingertips only grazed the rail as he fell backward.

His tumble stopped suddenly as it started, when a hot manacle locked around his wrist.

Will stood above him, one hand holding the box, the other holding Tate. Dark eyes blazed behind his shaggy hair. Heat from Will's hand travelled up Tate's arm and gathered in his chest. It was the first time in weeks that someone had touched him. Despite the severe expression on Will's face, despite being suspended mid-crash over the stairs, Tate felt oddly cared for.

"Thanks," he said.

Will's forearm corded as he pulled Tate upright. "Looking a little doughy there, Tater Tot."

"What?" Tate yanked his wrist free and his stomach sucked itself in, retreating from the pointy words. "Doughy?"

"Pale, like bread dough?" Will explained, as though it were the most obvious thing in the world.

"Good timing," Tate said, gripping the bannister. "Could've broken my neck."

Will grunted. "What a waste that would be."

"Where'd you come from, anyway?"

Will glanced over his shoulder. "Most people call it a door."

"Right."

Will leaned his hip against the rail, one hand steadying the box like it weighed precisely nothing. "What are you doing, trying to move this by yourself?"

"Didn't seem that heavy at first."

"They never do."

Will hauled the box up the rest of the stairs with grace. Bastard. Cymbria was right. Will was strong. And naturally thin. And good looking. Not quite handsome though, like his sister wasn't quite pretty. Both attractive, but in an androgynous way. It was Will's attitude that lent him a caustic masculinity.

Outside number nine, Tate dug in his pocket for his key.

"Need help setting it up?" Will asked.

"Think I can manage." Tate slid the key in the lock. "Thanks again. I owe you one. Really, if there's anything I can do for you, just ask. I'm happy to help."

Will's annoyance swarmed around them like a cloud of wasps. "If you wanna blow me that bad I won't stop you. But I'd just as soon leave it here, yeah?"

"Consider it left."

"Try not to stab yourself with a hammer." He clapped Tate on the back. "Later, Tater."

The door squealed shut behind Will, muting his footfalls down the stairs. Tate stood in the hall, the skin between his shoulder blades stinging. He listened for silver giggles or footsteps. Silence. Cymbria never did answer his question.

Inside the apartment, he opened the box and found all the parts and hardware he needed. Cymbria was right. He planned to use the desk to work. The work had already begun, in fact. He had plans.

Tate's eye wandered to his computer, currently sitting on the coffee table. Maybe he should contact Brad? That last conversation hadn't ended well. Tate did miss his brother and his nephews, but in a detached way. It didn't sit right. He wanted to miss them more. They were the only family he had.

The desk went together easy enough. As Tate tightened the final screw, he noticed the discoloration circling his wrist. Pink and tender, like a sunburn. In the shape of a handprint.

~

A knock at the door wrenched Tate out of his computer screen trance.

"Shit," he muttered, noting the late hour. He pushed away from the desk and shuffled over to the peephole. He yawned and opened the door.

Cymbria held up a plate of cinnamon rolls. "I made you a special treat."

The smell smashed into him, neither good nor bad, just overwhelming. He stared at the floor, searching for his words. "Cymbria, what the hell are you doing here?"

"You asked me to come by later."

"It's past midnight."

One eye narrowed as she pressed a finger to the bow of her upper lip. "Too late?"

"Well, yeah." He rubbed a hand over his face. "Or too early, depending on how you look at it. Jesus."

"Shoot, I've never been good with these..." the finger snap again. "Conventions."

Tate couldn't help noticing her chalky face, the purple shadows under her eyes, and the way her collarbones punched up too hard under her skin.

"Cymbria, are you okay?" he asked.

"I screwed up." She shoved a flour-streaked tendril of hair behind her ear. "When you visit, you're supposed to bring something. It's polite. But it took longer than I thought and time is like, something I don't really notice, and I do things without thinking them through, at least that's what Little Brother says, but he's wrong, because I think a lot, about all kinds of things, but they're always the wrong thing, you know?" She thrust the cinnamon rolls at him. "Anyway, here."

He took the plate and caught her arm as she pivoted to leave. "Wait."

Her face swiveled back to his, eyes bigger than ever. "I'm sorry, Tate."

Sorry. The sound of that word coming out of her mouth, the shape of it on her lips. It felt wrong. He never wanted her to say it again.

"Don't go," he said. "I was up anyway. Please, come in."

"I should leave you alone."

He pressed his thumb firmly into the hot crease of her elbow. "Come in."

She shivered as he pulled her across the threshold. Once inside, she slipped through his grasp, inch-by-inch, until her fingers glided over his. She clomped across the parquet floor in knee-high shitkickers, paired nicely with her white wife beater, like Johnny Walker and cigarettes. In between, a pink skirt flounced down her legs, and a matching ribbon secured her sloppy ponytail.

Goodbye Big Bird.

Hello Kitty.

"Wow." She stomped around his living room. "You've done a whole lotta nothing with the place.

"It's a good scotch," Tate said. "Doesn't need much. Just a few drops of water."

"You drink a lot of scotch?"

"Not as much as I've served. Before I came to Leighaven, I was a bartender."

Cymbria mimed a free pour. "That's always a sexy job in the movies."

"Yeah, a sexy consequence of an English degree."

Her mouth turned down. "You like to ruin the fantasy, don't you?"

"Constant source of disappointment, right here."

"Didn't mean it like that." She gave his arm a squeeze, a simple, tender touch that demanded nothing in return and stirred him more deeply than it should have. "Can I ask you something?"

"Go for it."

"It's personal," she warned.

He gave her a look. "I let you into my apartment in the middle of the night. Just ask."

"People quit their jobs all the time, Tate. You quit your whole life. Why?"

Tate paced back and forth for a long moment. "It's complicated. My brother thinks I've cracked up. That I'm selfish."

"Brothers are a chore sometimes."

"But it is selfish, isn't it? To suddenly blow town without telling anyone?"

Cymbria perched on the edge of his new desk, smoothing her cotton candy skirt over her knees. "A lot of things look sudden, Tate. Maybe some things are. But not people."

Tate continued pacing. "You know that content look people get on their faces when a person falls exactly in line? When all expectations are met and you've neatly slotted yourself into the space where they think you belong?"

Cymbria nodded, her eyes following him back and forth.

"My whole life," he said. "I've tried to be the guy my family and friends needed. I never stepped outside of the parameters they'd set. I'm a responsible business partner, a tireless worker, a last minute babysitter, a good brother, and by necessity the second best son, a place to crash, a bank to borrow from, a comic foil…whatever they wanted, I made it happen. I existed to put that look on their faces. I never questioned it."

Cymbria swung her crossed ankles. "They were happy. You thought you were happy too."

"That night, I realized my life wasn't even mine. I was a drone, performing as programmed. I saw a way out. So, I followed the trail."

"Into the woods," Cymbria said, catching his hand as he passed, arresting his pattern. They shared a moment of silence until the smell of cinnamon drove him to distraction.

He lifted the edge of the plastic on the plate. "It's a little late for me, but do you want one?"

"I already ate four." She clutched her stomach. "Can't help myself. Treats always make me happy. For a while, anyway."

Tate gazed at the pastries. "Sometimes that's enough."

"Are you writing something?" Cymbria touched the word-filled screen of his laptop.

Heat blasted into his ears as he snapped the screen down. "I was. Before you inappropriate neighbor'd me."

"A story?"

"Sort of, I'm not sure yet." He rubbed the back of his neck. Why was he telling her this? Why was she here? It was all so personal.

Cymbria hopped off his desk. "I love stories, so does Little Brother. For the longest time, we read the same old books over and over. But now, with the Internet, you can get anything you want, anything in the whole wide world!" She threw her arms out and twirled around his living room. Her skirt flew up, displacing cinnamon scented air and exposing her creamy thighs. Also, no bra.

He rubbed his eyes. "Can I ask you something now?"

"Want to play twenty questions? I love that game, even though Will hates it."

"Is there anything he doesn't hate?"

Cymbria's gaze dropped to the floor. "You don't like him."

Tate bobbled around all the words that wanted to go first. "I don't think he likes me. Or that I'm here, at Leighaven."

"He's a barky dog, but he'd never bite anyone who didn't deserve it." A softness crept into her expression as she defended her brother. "What was your question?"

"At the library, I found a book on the city's historical buildings. Leighaven was in there."

Cymbria's hands fluttered to her stomach. "So?"

"Wasn't much information. Stuff about the architecture and that it was built by Reinhold and Glory Leighaven in 1901."

"Guess there's not much to tell."

"Maybe, but I was interested, so I went down the street to land titles. Sweetie-pied a clerk half to death, hoping she could dig deeper into the building's history. Turns out Reinhold and Glory died just a few months after the building was finished, and ownership passed not to any family, but to The Leighaven Group, Reinhold's investment firm. In 1970, the Leighaven Group successfully lobbied the province to have the building declared a heritage sight, and they're still paying the taxes on it today out of a trust. Administered by Cymbria and William Leighaven."

"And we would have gotten away with it too, if it weren't for you pesky kids," she crowed. "Nice work, Scooby."

"I've been living here almost two months. We see each other almost every day. Why didn't you tell me your last name is Leighaven, or that you own this building?"

A dark look clouded her face. "Most times I feel like it owns us."

His heart squeezed out a run of irregular beats. "I get that."

She clutched his hands, her fingers threading through his wherever they found a gap. "Since we're confessing stuff, I may as well admit that when you emailed your application, I searched you up on the Google. I found an article on food and beverage spots. There was a picture, of you and your brother, in front of your bar. So, when you showed up last week…"

Tate pulled his hands free. "You expected a fat guy?"

"You've been preparing, Tate. Even if you didn't know it. You came here empty, just waiting to be filled up again. I knew you were the one to let in."

Cymbria didn't know Fat Tate. She didn't know that Fat Tate was a lot nicer than not Fat Tate. But Fat Tate was a doormat. Fat Tate couldn't say no. Fat Tate laughed it off but still cringed inside when his brother or his friends employed varied sobriquets like 'Tubs' or 'Tits' or the crowd favorite, 'Tater Tot', unwittingly resurrected by a certain lanky bastard in residence.

Cymbria dragged her finger down the middle of his chest. "I never expected Ken to turn up on my stoop."

"Ken?"

"Barbie's boyfriend. You know, blond and handsome." She scraped his hair back from his forehead. "I always wanted to be glamorous like Barbie."

On impulse, Tate tugged the pink ribbon on the back of her head. The bow slipped open and her hair tumbled down like a warm pelt. "You look better than any Barbie." His thumb brushed over her suddenly flushed cheek. But people were never sudden, were they?

Her hand closed around his wrist. "Tate, don't write about Leighaven."

"Why?"

"Because history is never over. It's never dead. You get real close and real quiet and you'll see it breathing."

Her queer-eyed stare held a plea, a warning, and something else. An affliction. Tate couldn't get a fix on her. Charming. Puzzling. Shifting to the left whenever he thought he had her pinned. A child with her goofy outfits. A woman, braless and knocking on his door in the small hours. Or a creature, with hidden fangs and dark eyes full of old secrets.

Cymbria Leighaven.

Her arm hooked around his neck and she pulled his mouth down to hers. They kissed with uncoordinated tongues, held breath, and clashing teeth. Everything terrible about first kisses, except it wasn't terrible at all. His hands slid under her shirt over the bare skin of her waist.

"Oh my god, you're hot," he said.

She giggled, not realizing he hadn't meant it colloquially. He boosted her back onto the desk and she pulled him between her legs, drawing him flush against her body. He fought the urge to recoil, like he would if he'd laid his hand on a hot stove.

"Cymbria, are you feeling okay?" he said. "You're really—"

"Shh."

Tate closed his eyes, falling into the taste of cinnamon, sugar, and butter. Everything good and satisfying in the world and all of it plated up so nicely on his new desk.

"Tell me what you want," she whispered.

Trick question? To hell with it. He ran his hands up her long legs, under her skirt. He hooked his thumbs into the sides of her panties. "I'd like to get you out of these."

He didn't know how long they kissed like that, his hands on her hips under her skirt. She wasn't craft beer, nor was she a cloying white zin. She was Tequila, straight up. Anejo. The good stuff you insist on but always regret.

Cymbria whimpered and wriggled against him. He tugged her panties down and wrestled them over her boots, lace snagging on steel hooks and chunky rubber tread.

"I'm sorry, Tate. I'm so sorry."

"Stop…saying that," he said between kisses, scalding his mouth on her neck and along her shoulder. His hand inched up her inner thigh, until he scorched his fingertips on slippery flesh that turned his brain to soup and his cock to stone.

"It's too soon," she whispered. "I shouldn't…it's too soon."

His hand stilled between her legs. "Want me to stop?"

"Mmm, and would you?" She rocked against his hand. "If I asked you to, right now?"

This was not the time for an interrogation. He was in a far too honest place. *You have questions? Ask away. Don't be shy. Let's get personal.*

Yes. Within three minutes of making her acquaintance, he'd wanted to fuck this bug-eyed weirdo blind. Yes. Her warning about Leighaven chilled him on a basement level of himself he didn't understand. And yes. If she asked him to stop now he would but...

"Barely," he whispered and caught her mouth under his again.

She'd started this. She had. Hadn't she? And now he needed it, needed her, like all the light in the universe would gutter out and he'd freeze to death in the dark if she were to push him away.

Her laughter rippled down his throat as she reached between them. He was in her hand. Then he was in her. Tate flinched as intense heat gloved him. Was she full of lava or something? This wasn't normal. She had a fever. She sure as hell looked sick. Whatever it was, he hoped it wasn't contagious.

Speaking of contagious. No condom. This was beyond idiotic.

Sweat slicked down his back under his shirt. Cymbria clawed at his shoulders and those awful boots scraped his hips. The desk creaked. His socks slipped on the floor. Her hair caught between their mouths, tying their tongues together.

The bartender always gets laid. An embarrassingly true stereotype. However, losing almost one hundred pounds had a curious effect on his game. He got more looks for sure, more flirty smiles, arm petting, and phone numbers scratched on napkins slid across the bar at him from the insanely hot Stella-from-the-bottle Thursday Girls that never would have looked at him twice before. But when it came to the women he genuinely wanted to get to know better, they were less receptive than they'd been when he was pudgy. Ergo, the last sex he'd had was over a year and fifty pounds ago. A long time. And now it was too soon. Too late.

"Cymbria."

"Wait." She pushed her forehead hard against his. "Almost there."

Distraction. Delay. Provincial capitals, the Greek alphabet, open gut surgery. But for whatever reason, an image of Will formed in his mind. Prince Charmless, with a morbidly obese chip on his stupid, perfect shoulders. Will, with the same pale skin, long limbs, and black velvet eyes full of I-know-something-you-don't.

Tate buried his face in Cymbria's hot neck as he came. Not a second later, she tensed around him. And the noise that came out of her. No exaggeration. The woman roared.

Murmuring nonsense, they bumbled their way to the bedroom.

"I tried not to...thought maybe just touching you a little...but you feel so good." Words dropped like wilted flower petals. "Couldn't help it...did you mind?"

"Stop talking," Tate said. "And I'll show you how much I mind."

He stripped her like the Barbie doll she'd always wanted to be and they fell onto the white duvet. A slower pace, yet not a moment to spare for sober second thought. In the dark she clutched him, pleading, repeating, a chant, a mantra.

"Please, Tate. Please let me...just let me...please..."

"Yes," he whispered into her soft, wet mouth, holding her hips against his. The question didn't matter when there existed only one conceivable answer.

~

Concentric circles. Nine rows of nine. Tate blinked at the ceiling tiles, pink ripples in the early light. Blinking felt like an accomplishment. Now, if he could only turn his head. The sound of his hair dragging over the pillow was like wire bristles on wooden planks. His neck muscles felt inflamed and tight as they rolled his leaden skull to the left. Toward an empty pillow. Another blink.

"Cymbria?" he croaked, not really expecting an answer, not really expecting the gummy meat of his throat to produce sound.

He shambled out of the bedroom. The only evidence that it hadn't been an acid-etched hallucination was the plate of cinnamon rolls on the desk. That, and the big bastard of a sex hangover that couldn't have been worse if he'd downed a fifth of Patrón. The parquet floor went swirly. His stomach lurched.

"Ugh."

Cymbria. She'd been an animal, a lion. She'd run him down and ripped him open. Even as she ate him alive, his body reported only pleasure. Metaphor or not, it freaked him out.

Tate rubbed the glue out of his eyes. Shower. The most glorious idea of all time. Hot water. Soap. Yes.

He pulled the shower curtain around the inner circumference of the freestanding tub. Water hissed. Tate stood under the spray, listening to the downpour hit the bottom of the tub in a steady rumble.

The warm water turned to freezing rain when an outline of a face slowly pushed in on the opaque shower curtain. Two shadowy hands pressed in on either side of the face. Tate yanked the curtain aside. White tiles, toilet, pedestal sink, painted pipes. His towel on the rack.

Slick plastic slapped against his back.

Tate whipped around, slipping on the enamel and taking the curtain down with him. He hit his head on the edge of the tub. Black fog obscured his vision and the pattering of water on the curtain exploded into gunfire. In the midst of it, he heard giggling. Silver bullets.

Hastily dressed in sweat pants and a t-shirt, Tate fought off waves of nausea from the throbbing gull's egg on his head as he stalked down the dim hallway and around the corner. Two doors, one on either side of the corridor. The kids lived in one of these units. Every time they disappeared on the third floor.

His knock echoed in the empty hall. He listened for movement, watched for a shift in the light creeping through the gap between the door and the floor. He knocked again. Waited. Crossed the hall. More knocking, listening and watching. Someone had to be home. Tate raised his fist, prepared to bang on the door. He paused. Maybe there was a better way to do this than terrorizing potentially innocent neighbors.

On the ground floor, Tate didn't knock. He shoved the office door open. Two near-identical faces fixed on him from opposite ends of the room. Will behind the desk, hands frozen mid-stich on his needles, and Cymbria in the corner kitchen, yawning as she twirled a spoon in a mug.

"Oh my god, Tate!" Cymbria dropped her spoon and snatched up a white tea towel.

"The kids," Tate snapped. "Where do they live? I want to speak to their parents."

Will resumed his knitting. "You know you're bleeding from the head, right? Like a medium amount?"

Tate touched his temple and his fingers came away scarlet.

"What happened?" Cymbria skittered over, pressing the warm towel to the cut.

"They broke into my apartment, at least the girl did. I heard her."

Will glanced at Cymbria. "You sure, Tater? This building makes a lot of weird noises. Old pipes and what not."

"It wasn't the fucking pipes, Will. I was in the shower. I saw a face through the curtain. I heard them. That damn creepy giggling."

"Come sit, okay?" Cymbria guided him to an armchair and knelt at his feet, keeping the towel on his head. "They didn't break in, Tate. I left the door unlocked behind me. I shouldn't have, but I didn't want to wake you."

Tate felt Will's gaze incinerating them both.

"I'm sure she didn't mean any harm," Cymbria said, gripping Tate's hand. "She just likes to play. If she'd known you were hurt."

Will strolled over, giving Tate's shoulder an ungentle nudge. "You don't waste any fucking time, do you?"

Tate stood, looking Will in the eye. "That's none of your business."

Cymbria wedged herself between them. "Will, don't."

"Don't what?" Will glared her down. "Don't spread 'em for number nine?"

"Hey, that's enough," Tate said.

"You really wanna get into it with me, Tater Tot?" Will snarled so ferociously that Tate actually stepped back. So Cymbria wasn't the only poorly domesticated animal at Leighaven.

"Shh, there's no need for that." Cymbria cupped Will's face in her hands, stroking his cheeks with her thumbs. "No need, no need..." Will jerked his chin out of her grasp. Vertigo clapped Tate right back into the chair. Cymbria turned to him. "Let's get you upstairs. You need to rest, and you should eat something."

Will snorted. "Like that's going to help? Damage is done, Little Sister."

Cymbria quailed under her brother's scorn. Tate didn't understand. Where did this crabby, son-of-a-bitch get off, shaming a grown woman like he would a misbehaving child?

Didn't help that Cymbria was dressed like a damn toddler in overalls and a purple t-shirt. Tate found it hard to reconcile that just a few hours ago he'd been inside her. Hard to believe her cinnamon-sweet mouth had dripped onto him filth that would've made a roughneck blush.

She also looked a hell of a lot healthier than she had last night. Her cheeks pink and plump, eyes sparkling, hair shiny. Now that he was paying attention, it looked like whatever had been draining her had latched on to Will. Bruised circles bagged under his eyes and where his sister's skin was heavy cream, his had the bluish tint of skim milk.

It was the first time he'd seen both Leighavens in the same room. Maybe it was the concussion, but together, they were even more bizarre. Like aliens zipped up in humanish skin. Passing, but barely.

"Please, don't be cross," she said softly to Will, her thin arms flexing as she gathered handfuls of his shirt. "I'm not as strong as you are."

"We'll talk about this later," Will said, and then he turned to Tate. "I'll sort out your trespasser problem. Now go home, get some sleep, and lock your goddamn door."

"Tell the parents to get a leash on their kids. Next time I'm calling the police." Tate took several lurching steps down the hall. When he looked back, Will leaned out of the office door, like a frost glazed bottle of vodka rolling out of an open freezer.

"I told you to stay away from her," he said.

Tate bobbed his head. Acknowledgment, rather than agreement. The truth was, Will had never told him any such thing.

The stairs took forever. His pulse boomed in his temples and he kept losing his balance. In his apartment, he searched every corner, cupboard and closet. Satisfied he was alone, he noodled into his desk chair. The blood on the side of his head itched. The plate of cinnamon rolls was within arm's reach. When he peeled off the wrap, the spicy smell hit him and his dick semi-hardened in his sweats. After last night, he was surprised the thing wasn't dead.

He picked up a pastry and took a bite, chewing slowly. Saliva flooded into his mouth and his stomach shivered. What was she? A freak in the sack. A god in the kitchen. He stared at the handful of heaven in his palm, one bite missing. If he ate any more, what was to stop him from eating them all?

With a flump they slid into the trashcan. Fat Tate would be appalled over the waste, but mostly, over the rudeness of it. How much of his weight problem was gluttony, and how much was his crippling desire to please?

Staring at those cinnamon rolls in the trashcan, Tate couldn't pretend he wasn't conflicted, but he'd made the decision. He'd had his taste and now they were gone.

~

It had to happen sooner or later. He'd been lucky to avoid it as long as he had, but after nearly a week, Tate's uppance had come. Outside the laundry room, around the bend in the hall, he heard a series of scrapes and thumps. He poured detergent into the drum, shut the lid, and started the machine. A diffuse glow bled around the corner of the hallway.

Tate hadn't explored this part of the basement. Instead of another hallway, he found a large open space with three massive boilers, a modern electrical panel, shelves loaded with cardboard boxes, and Will, dragging a rolled up carpet over the concrete floor.

"I expected skeletons," said Tate.

Black eyes glittered in the low light. "Say what?"

"Decent creep factor down here. Just seems like there should be skeletons."

Will grunted. "Make yourself useful, yeah? Grab the other end."

Fibers from the cut edge dug into Tate's hands. "What is this?"

"Old stuff I ripped out before you moved in. Last tenant ruined it. Never got around to feeding it to the bin."

Tate's arms strained. "You were going to move this yourself?"

"See anyone else lining up to help? Little Sister's more about the play than the work, as you might've noticed," Will said with a pointed look. "C'mon."

Tate puffed as they lugged the carpet down the hall and through the stairwell door. "Thanks for dealing with the kids for me. No sign of them since that day."

"They were just having fun, Tater." Will took the first few stairs, pulling the roll with him. "Don't you remember what it was like to be a kid?"

"I never broke into people's homes."

"They've been at Leighaven their whole lives. They think of the entire building as their home."

"Are they related to you?"

Will stopped halfway up the stairs, abruptly dropping his end and letting the full weight of the roll rest against Tate. "Could say that."

"Uh…Will, could you maybe…" Tate groaned under the strain.

"Jesus, Tater Tot." Will picked up the carpet, tucking it under one long arm. "We gotta work on your upper body strength. There, just give'r another shove. That's it."

They manhandled the carpet out of the stairwell, down the main floor hall and out the back door. Together, they tipped the roll into the dumpster. A thick plume of dust shimmered in the sunset.

"Thanks," Will panted.

"Anytime," Tate said, and surprisingly, meant it. It felt good to be useful. He had scratches all over his arms, but the sting was satisfying. In his old life, he'd resented being the only one hauling a sledge loaded with several people's burdens. But with Will in harness right next to him, pulling just as hard, it was different.

Will braced an arm against Leighaven's exterior sandstone, hanging his head. A faint wheeze accompanied the outline of his ribs heaving through his t-shirt.

"You okay?" Tate asked.

"Fine…just…dandy." Will flipped his head back. Sweat gleamed in the hollow of his throat and the sinking sun deepened the shadows around his eyes. "What're you looking at?"

"Not a thing. D'you want to come up for a beer?"

The combination of his greyish pallor and lopsided smirk made Will look downright sinister. "Don't think it's a good idea, Tater."

"Okay." Tate tried not to look disappointed.

"I'm not saying no," Will added. "I'm just…saying."

"Right." Tate paused. "But, I'm just saying, the last ghoul-faced Leighaven to walk through my door walked out looking like a million bucks."

Will's eyes narrowed to the size of regular eyes. "Man, you got a hell of a cheek on you."

"Are you coming or what?" Tate opened the door and stepped into the gloomy hallway.

~

"It's not that I hate kids." Tate reached into the fridge, fingers closing around two cold glass necks. "I have two nephews."

"Angels, I suppose?" Will produced a pocketknife and pried the caps off the bottles.

They sat down on opposite ends of the pink sofa. Tate took a pull from his beer, letting it drain deliciously thick down his throat. Usually, he couldn't justify the calories, but Russian stout was created for Monday nights with awkward company.

"My nephews are a lot like my brother," Tate said. "So they're kind of awful, but great, too. They laugh until they fall down, they're noisy, messy, and when they hug you, it's like getting tackled by a rhino. They go at life so hard, you know?"

"Sometimes."

"But the kids here, they aren't like that. They're sly. Almost feral."

Will said nothing. They stared straight ahead at an empty yellow wall, filling the silence with quiet gulps of stout while dusk barged through the window and fouled the apartment with shadows. Within minutes, Tate couldn't make out much more than a silhouette of his guest. The silhouette tilted its head and Tate felt dilated pupils fix on him like spotlights. Or the exact opposite. Focused beams of zero illumination. Notlights.

"Saw a thing on TV once, about feral kids." Will's smoky voice curled through the darkness. "Babies ditched in abandoned tenements in Ukraine."

"Scary."

The shadow man shrugged. "These kids develop differently. They can see in the dark, smell a storm two days

127

away, and hear a spider walking on its web. They learn how to forage and stay warm. Some of them even figure out how to trap live meat."

"No kidding?"

"By the time they get 'rescued', they're more animal than human. They've got a totally different nature. Can't be civilized. So, they get locked away."

Tate downed the last mouthful of stout, no longer cold. "You think they're better off living like animals? That Remus and Romulus stuff is a myth, Will. Kids left on their own, even if they can find food, they'll eventually get sick or hurt. It's not like the fairy tales."

"Where d'you think fairy tales start? Someone lost in the woods. Maybe they curl up under a tree and die, or maybe they keep going. The will to survive is powerful. Especially in kids. Powerful enough to bend the fucking universe."

Tate wondered. Was there a situation here? Abuse or neglect? Was Will telling him to leave well enough alone? Leighaven creaked and popped around them. Pipes juddered as water was called forth. A police siren careened by on the street below. Tate peered blindly across the couch at a shadow he suspected could see just fine. Something about being watched when he couldn't see unnerved him beyond his tolerance. He reached over to switch on the desk lamp.

Will hissed, his hand flying up to shield his eyes.

Tate held up his bottle. "Want another?"

"Why not." Will drained the last of his beer and scratched his finger over the pink upholstery of the couch. "This thing."

"What's wrong with it?"

"Ugly as hell. I could make you an afghan. How d'you feel about grey?"

"Swell." Tate took the empties to the kitchen. "What's with the knitting, anyway? Not many guys are into it."

Will didn't fire a smartass round from his retort cannon, but rather, stared at his hands, resting palms up on his legs. "Like how it feels is all. Life is hard. Yarn is always soft. What am I doing here, man? Seriously."

"Seriously?" Tate pulled a loaf of bread out of the fridge. "I'm going to make sandwiches. You hungry?"

Will's eyes gleamed in their deep hollows. "Starved."

"Good. I'll fix you up."

"You would offer it just like that."

"A sandwich?"

"Jesus, Tater, develop some trust issues like a normal person, yeah?"

Tate shrugged. "I've got turkey."

"Cheese?"

"Nope."

"Course not."

Tate made the sandwiches. Lettuce, tomato, and mustard. No mayonnaise. Whole grain bread. Between that, the stout, and the turkey, it was Carb Christmas.

"Call it an olive branch." Tate offered Will a fresh bottle and a sandwich. "I'd like to get right with you. I'm sorry about Cymbria."

Will rolled his eyes. "Did you rape her?"

Tate nearly coughed out his first bite. "Is that what you think?"

"If I did, you'd be in the dumpster, rolled up in that rug." Will set his bottle on the coffee table and chomped into his sandwich. "You got nothing to be sorry for. It's called seduction, Tater. Believe me, you didn't stand a chance."

"She told you?"

"Didn't have to. I know her."

Tate slouched back on the couch. "I've stopped by the office every day, sometimes twice a day, but she hasn't been around. I think she's avoiding me."

Will chuckled. "Someone's got a crush on Little Sister."

"Laugh it up," Tate muttered into his bottle before taking a drink. "Why d'you call each other that? Little Sister. Little Brother."

"Family joke. She's smaller, I'm younger – by about ten minutes."

"Twins?"

"Hatched from the same meatsack, or so says the paperwork. Not that there's much of it. I suspect the adoption arrangements were shady as fuck, but fat cats have a way of writing their own rules, don't they? They wanted kids so they went out and bought a pair. Like shoes."

"You're not close with your folks?"

"Gave us their name, this mausoleum, and not much else." A scowl swept over Will's face. "They're gone, now. Dusted."

"Mine too."

"You miss 'em?"

"All the time."

"You're tight with your brother though."

"I thought so. But could you walk out on Cymbria like I walked out on Brad?"

Will shook his head. "She'd hunt me down and drag me back. Little Sister's stronger than she looks."

"No shit." Tate said, catching his tongue too late. "That came out wrong."

Will's hot hand clamped around the back of Tate's neck. "Relax, man. Probably seemed weird, me going berserk over you and her. Thing is, Cym's got impulse control issues. Does things without thinking them through. She's all I have, Tater. And I protect what's mine."

Protect her from what? From unsafe sex with strangers? Was it a pattern? Will did seem more pissed than surprised at the whole thing. Tate made a mental note to get himself tested for everything from the clap to SARS.

"To family." Tate raised his bottle and Will clanked his against it. A shrill twittering bounced off the walls, floor and ceiling. A moment of silence and the twittering repeated.

"Speaking of our resident succubus." Will dug in his pocket and pulled out a phone.

Tate hadn't heard a phone ring in almost two months. And now, to have one shrieking in close proximity? He could confidently say it was the most god-awful sound in the universe.

"Uh huh…upstairs with number nine…yeah, really…you should come up…just get your ass up here…see you in a few."

Tate shoved Will's shoulder hard with the heel of his hand. "What're you doing?"

"Getting you out of your own goddamn way." Will jammed the phone back in his pocket. The movement dragged the waistband of his jeans down exposing a taut slice of abdomen sweeping like a snowdrift to the crest of his hipbone. "Cym's a tricky bird, Tater. Never gonna fly into your cage just because you leave the door open. Has to be something in there she can't say no to."

"Like what?"

"Like me."

Tate sucked back the bottom third of his beer and banged the bottle down on the coffee table. "William Leighaven, you are the devil."

Will flashed an honest-to-god smile that promised only sin. Lots of it.

Cymbria waltzed in without knocking. Tate stared at her outfit. Flip-flops, basketball shorts, and a Hawaiian shirt knotted beneath her breasts, exposing a long arc of midriff. She'd changed the game on him again. This wasn't tequila. This was Malibu rum, pineapple juice, and coke. Trailer park colada.

Tate wrenched his eyes upward. "Hi."

She ignored him, homing in on her brother. "This is the last place I expected to find you."

Will shrugged. "Guess I know when I'm beaten."

She glanced at Tate and then back to Will. "But you said—"

"Forget what I said." Will braced one hand on the back of the couch and pressed his eyes shut for a moment. "We both know it's too late."

Cymbria's features melted into something like sadness. Something like grief. She walked up to her brother, held his head in her hands and burrowed her fingers in his hair. "You look awful. You need this."

Will opened his eyes and stared into hers. "I had some."

"A scrap here? A crumb there? That's not enough."

Tate stepped forward. "Hey, if you want another sandwich, there's plenty of—"

Will thwacked him with a glare so hateful it seemed to form a dark halo around his head, sharpening the angles of his gaunt face. Minutes ago, they'd been having their first real conversation over Russian stout. Will almost seemed to be enjoying himself. But with Cymbria's arrival, Little Brother was back to grouch city.

She pressed her cheek to Will's. "You're running hot."

"Why do you think I called you up here? It's time."

"Okay then." Cymbria looked over her shoulder at Tate. Her lips parted slightly and her tongue flicked between her teeth like a snake tasting the air. "Miss me?"

Tate took a reflexive step back. "Just wanted to see how you are."

"Dandy as a dandelion." She slithered over and dragged her nail over the scab on his forehead, sending threads of fire down his spine. "Does it hurt?"

"This helps." Tate's arms reached out of their own accord, finding the hot skin of her waist. Maybe it was the stout, or perhaps it was what he'd come to think of as the Leighaven Effect. Prolonged exposure to the building and its management had a way of heightening the senses while rounding off the edges of reality. Tate didn't care anymore that something massively odd was afoot. Or that Will was still glaring from the other side of the room as his sister steered Tate onto the couch and straddled his lap.

"Don't you want some?" Cymbria asked, looking over her shoulder.

Will shook his head. "You first."

With a smile she turned back to Tate. "Little Brother likes to watch."

Sweat beaded along his hairline. He was on the wrong side of their language barrier. The smoldering woman-creature in his arms squirmed closer. He forced himself to let go of the need to understand, and when she kissed him, Tate knew he was lost.

Her lips left his, only to yank his shirt off, and then they were back, on his mouth, ears, face, and neck. He unknotted her Hawaiian shirt, pulled it off and threw it away. Her naked skin threw off a blast of nearly unbearable heat, and Tate wanted nothing more than to burn his mouth on her nearly flat chest and stomach. All the way down.

Then another pair of hands glided over Cymbria's bare shoulders. Tate could only watch as Will grabbed Cymbria's jaw, wrenched her head around and kissed her hard. Cymbria leaned back into her brother, returning his kiss, even as she rocked her hips against Tate's hard-on.

"Fuck, you guys are so weird," Tate groaned, but they didn't seem to hear him over the ravening noises in their throats.

Will slung his arm across Cymbria's collarbones, locking her in place as he kissed her deep and deeper. Until it could no longer be called a kiss, and Tate no longer felt aroused but drugged. His limbs grew numb and heavy. His breath came in labored gusts. The conduit of Will and Cymbria's joined mouths glowed white, even as the dark chasm of their hunger yawned open.

Cymbria flattened her palms against Tate's chest. It burned like a branding iron. He gasped, raising his weak arms to push her away. She grabbed him around the neck and crushed him to her, toasting his face on her breasts. Under her skin, he felt the rhythmic contraction of muscle. Her whole body acted as a pump, drawing not blood but something even more vital from the living pulp of him, and shotgunning it into Will.

Tate found himself thrown back as Will hauled Cymbria off his lap and pushed her down on the sofa beneath him. Tate rolled to the floor, banging his shoulder on the coffee table. Through bleary eyes, he watched their passionate embrace turn brutal.

Will kept his mouth clamped hard over Cymbria's as she whimpered and struggled. Her wrists bruised and her skin blanched as she fought, but Will held her down, appearing to grow stronger as she weakened. Finally, her body went limp and her big eyes rolled back before closing. Will broke the kiss. Then he stroked Cymbria's hair until the last drops of tension drained from her mottled face and she fell solidly unconscious.

Tate couldn't believe the difference when Will slid off the couch to sit on the floor. The heroin addict pallor was gone, replaced by the pearly glow of health, and his eyes glittered like chipped onyx.

Will turned to him with that devil's smile. "You're not looking so hot, Tater tot."

"Wha…" Tate couldn't even form the one-word question.

"She wasn't lying." Will took a deep contented breath. "What little you got tastes damn fine. I haven't felt this good in decades."

Tate tried to lift his head. Might as well have been a mountain. He glanced over at Cymbria's blue-tinged skin and purple lips. "Is she…"

Will responded with one of his withering looks. "Like I'd shove my only family in the proverbial oven for you?"

"Then why?"

Will grazed his knuckles over the bruise forming on Tate's shoulder. "Little Sister likes you an awful lot. Would've hated herself for killing you, and I can't have her hurt like that." Tate's heart struggled to pound the adrenaline through his body as Will's face moved in closer. "I like you too, Tater. At least I like the person I think you could be. But I could still drain you dead without losing a speck of sleep over it. So the question becomes – what am I gonna do with you?"

The question sank into the murky grog of Tate's mind. He tried to move his fingers and found he couldn't. He attempted to speak, but his voice wouldn't come. His pulse slowed. His eyes refused to focus. Death wasn't as unappealing as it ought to have been, and he'd already left so much behind, it would be easy to drift away. In spite of all that, Tate wasn't ready.

"Good choice," Will said, sliding on top of him. "Try to relax. This might feel strange. For both of us."

Strange was one way of putting it. Strangely repellent. Strangely compelling. Will's mouth tasted like butter and cinnamon, like Cymbria, and his wiry body crushed Tate into the floor. Whatever the mechanism, skin contact seemed to get the job done, but slowly. Kissing – or fucking, for that matter – created a direct pipeline. Typically, the flow went from the prey to predator. Now, Will forced it in the opposite direction, creating violent turbulence. Tate gagged as it gushed into him and tried to pull away but Will bit into his tongue, forcing his mouth wide open.

Luminous energy filled the chambers of Tate's heart and
lit up his blood. Strength flooded back into his limbs and he
moaned when his revived erection pushed against Will's. It
made sense now. This was more than their fuel source. It
was a narcotic, an aphrodisiac, an elevator, a regenerator. In
its clutches, pain, regret, morality, and identity were
rendered meaningless. The cries of extinct animals.

Tate ran his hands under Will's shirt feeling his skin heat
to a blaze. Like a shot of ice cold Chopin pouring fire down
his throat. The kind of vodka you sip alone, not because you
have a problem, but because it's just that special.

Will broke the seal of their mouths and panted against
Tate's neck, the harsh rasp of worn out machinery. Tate
didn't know what else to do for Will, so he held him.

Until a little girl's laugh rang out in the hallway.

Pushing Will off, Tate scrambled to his feet, wincing as
his teeth scraped his bitten tongue. Will propped himself up
and licked away the blood trickling out of his mouth. He
looked even worse than he had earlier in the evening. Skull
clearly defined under his bleached skin. Cheeks flushed with
sickness rather than health. Death boiled over.

The girl's laugh echoed through the stairwell.

"Those kids, what are they?" Tate asked.

"Dreams," Will muttered.

"You mean ghosts?"

Will's glazed eyes sharpened. "No ghosts here. Little
Sister and I, we clean our plates."

Rage simmered in Tate's rejuvenated veins. "There are
no other tenants in this building."

"Think of it as serial monogamy."

"Or serial murder."

Will uttered a weak laugh. "Does a wolf murder a
rabbit?"

"Is that what you are? Wolves?"

"Wish I knew. Unfortunately, this ain't a fairy story. There's no woodsman coming to the rescue, or an evil witch with a candy house, or a moldy old book with all the answers. Sometimes the breadcrumbs don't lead anywhere."

"They led me here."

"And it's a good job more people don't know the way. Otherwise, we'd have a queue out the door. Don't act like you don't know."

Tate knew. Sex was only a word, a crude act that couldn't begin to describe the pleasure of that metaphysical energy dialysis. But that's not all it was. He felt something that night with Cymbria. He felt it tonight in the midst of their fucked up three-way, and again, just now, on the floor. He felt cared for. Of course, that was part of their game, wasn't it? Seduction.

"That's all I am to you? A meal?"

"Christ, don't push it." Will managed to sound dangerous despite his exhaustion.

"You wanna hear something that makes you feel like a special snowflake? Listen to your heart, yeah? The fact that it's beating right now makes you special. The fact that I've never, in over a hundred years, done what I just did for you makes you fucking special."

Tate stared at his shoes. "She said I was the right one to let in."

"But not the right time. You're too thin."

Tate's hands covered his stomach. "What?"

"Your soul, dumbass. It's emaciated. Saw it the second I laid eyes on you. Christ knows how long you've been starving yourself of everything good in life." Will's bruised eyes softened. "Cym promised me it would work out, that she could fatten you up. I may be a grouchy son-of-a-bitch, but there's not much I wouldn't do to make her happy."

Tate swallowed hard. "Then let me stay."

Will shook his head. "Go back to your brother and your bar. Watch your disgusting nephews grow up. Do it right this time. Live the life you want. Write that novel. Drink with your friends. Fall in love. Break some hearts. Make a big fat feast of your existence. And when you're stuffed so full you're tearing at the seams, then you'll come home to us. To Leighaven."

Tate shook his head. "But I can't leave the two of you, not like this."

"You can." Will tensed like a feverish panther. "Or I'll take back everything I just gave you with interest. I'll have you in ways you can't even imagine, and I know a part of you wants it, but timing is everything, Tater."

Tate shoved his hands in his pockets and his fingers clutched his car keys. All he needed to escape. If only he wanted to.

Will didn't wait for a final answer. He dragged himself onto the couch where he curled his body around Cymbria's, kissed her ear, closed his eyes, and joined her in a death-like slumber. Twin corpses. Babes in the woods. But instead of a cadaverous chill, they radiated heat so intense it turned the entire apartment into an oven. If Tate stayed much longer, the Leighavens might literally cook him for dinner.

In the hall, Tate heard the tramp of little feet. Dreaming familiars. Echoes of what they'd once been. Human children. Feral and starved, their will to survive bent the universe. Transformed them into something you couldn't bottle. A strange brew.

Tate pulled on his shirt and left number nine. He dawdled down the stairs, past the office, through the heavy front door, and jogged up the block to his car without so much as a glance over his shoulder. When the time came, he wouldn't need a trail of crumbs to find his way back to Leighaven. He had history here, and history never died. No matter how dark, or how still, if you got real close and real quiet, you'd hear it breathing.

~

A Ballad for Wheezy Barnes

~

Wheezy Barnes leaned on his mop, watching his streaky Z pattern evaporate off the men's room floor. Custodial work at the Calgary Stampede wasn't what most people classified as a dream job. But Wheezy Barnes loved two things, and the Stampede provided him with daily servings of both. He breathed deep, scalded his lungs with disinfectant, and consulted his watch. 4:25 p.m. Splendid timing.

Wheezy slipped behind the Nashville North tent and picked his way over the electrical cords snaking across the pavement to where a gap in the side of the tent allowed him a direct line of sight to the stage. The dense crowd chanted her name. Celebrity impersonators were a big draw at the Stampede, but no one packed 'em in like Tammy Whynot. Wheezy hopped on an oil drum, struck a match, and lit his one and only unfiltered cigarette of the day.

The music started. It was time.

Tammy bounced out of the wings, an angel in denim and rhinestones. In her mid-forties, at least twenty years older than Wheezy, but radiating a youthful lack of guile. A dimple punctuated her cheek when she smiled, and Wheezy imagined pressing his thumb into that dimple, holding her smile in place.

"Howdy!" Tammy said and tipped her white Stetson to the band.

Wheezy crushed his cigarette against the sole of his sneaker. Seven years since he'd first heard her sing. Seven years, and nothing had changed.

Mopping up social blight at the Stampede was Wheezy's vacation from his regular gig, selling high-grade marijuana to an exclusive clientele of aging hippies. But Wheezy wasn't a drug dealer, not really. He'd inherited the family business, that was all. And as the hippies got older, their demand for pot was surpassed by a need for custodial services. Windows, floors, light housekeeping. An evolution that suited Wheezy just fine.

Tammy yodeled across the stage in a spot-on imitation of Dolly Parton. Wheezy popped a Pepto-Bismol tablet, leaned back and closed his eyes. Her voice soothed his stomach. For seven years he'd planned his breaks, and his acid reflux, to coincide with her performances. Sometimes he fantasized about meeting her. One day, if he got close enough, just maybe, his angel would touch his hand.

A guitar lick finished the set and Tammy blew kisses at the crowd. "I'll be back tomorrow, but if any of y'all are going to the Winterbourne shindig tonight, I'll see you there!"

Wheezy sat up. His dangling feet thudded against the drum. A private performance at one of the chuck wagon parties? Tammy never gave private performances. He couldn't help imagining: intimate venue, small crowd, soft light. She'd be so close. For seven years he'd loved Tammy at a distance. Just maybe, it was time.

Except he had to work. A problem, with one potential solution.

Wheezy found Spencer in the usual place: rescuing pop cans out of the garbage bin and throwing them into the recycling bin.

"Hi, Wheezy," Spencer said without looking up. "Eight, nine, ten…"

"Spencer, I need you to cover my shift tonight."

Spencer froze. "The midway?"

"Yes."

"All by myself? I don't like the midway at nighttime, Wheezy."

Spencer's gloved fists curled up to his chest. If his hands started to flap, it was over.

"Please," said Wheezy, reaching up to squeeze Spencer's forearms. "It's only this once."

Spencer shuddered, and slowly lowered his hands. "Okay, Wheezy."

Wheezy picked another can out of the garbage. "Eleven," he said, tossing it at the recycling bin. It bounced off the rim and hit the pavement.

~

Wheezy squinted as silver fire blazed from the spurs of Tammy's pink boots. The fringe on her vest danced like hundreds of energetic fingers playing piano. Her eyelashes and breasts were clearly mass-produced. But the way the corner of her mouth chased that elusive dimple…*One of a kind*, thought Wheezy.

"Howdy, y'all!" Tammy trilled when the last chord of 'Long Time Gone' faded. "Now's the time to grab a cold one, folks. About to get mighty hot in here!"

The opening riff of 'I Love Rock 'n Roll' blasted. Tammy sang and worked the stage in a series of slinky moves Wheezy had no names for. Growling out the chorus, she ripped her vest and skirt right off. Her new outfit consisted of a white bikini top and short-shorts, both studded with rhinestones. Wheezy eyed the discarded vest and skirt, crumpled like dead animals. This was not his Tammy.

One song gyrated into another. Wheezy couldn't look away. Tammy left the stage and shimmied through the crowd. His stomach cannonballed into his throat when she kicked out her leg to straddle some jerk in ironed jeans and a backwards cowboy hat. Wheezy dug in his pocket for a Pepto-Bismol. This was definitely not his Tammy.

At some point, Wheezy fell into a chair. All around him the Wednesday night version of the Winterbourne party descended into naked debauchery. He didn't want to stay, but he'd forgotten how to leave. At a table in front of him, a woman slithered to her knees, attempting to give her companion a blowjob. Jesus.

Wheezy lurched from his chair, desperate to escape. Near the exit, he spotted Spencer. Spencer did not look happy. Hunched over, hands braced on his thighs, Spencer appeared on the verge of atomic fission.

Wheezy ran.

"Wheezy…Wheezy," Spencer panted. "I need…he was yelling…"

"Slow down." Wheezy pressed his hands on the middle of Spencer's back. "Take three deep breaths."

Spencer immediately calmed, thank God. He followed the instructions to the letter, and straightened up.

"Now," Wheezy said. "Tell me what happened."

As always, Spencer focused on a spot just over Wheezy's left shoulder. "A man who smelled like cigarettes grabbed my shirt. He told me to clean up the shitstorm in Tammy Whynot's trailer. I told him I had to find my supervisor. I tried to ask what's a shitstorm. He yelled things about my mother – I think he was telling lies, Wheezy. I think he's a bad man."

Wheezy nodded, careful not to make eye contact. "He was definitely telling lies, Spence. Did you find the supervisor?"

Spencer shook his head, opening a possibility.

Only supervisors were supposed to handle the talent.

He could get fired for this.

Did it matter?

Tammy's dirty performance had flattened him. Nothing made sense. Wheezy Barnes loved two things. But he could clean anywhere. In a few days he'd be back mucking out gutters and selling pot to arthritic hippies. There was only one Tammy though, only one angel with a skittish dimple in her cheek. She was the reason he was here, at the party, at the Stampede, and she was slipping away.

"Don't tell the supervisor, Spence," Wheezy said. "I'll take care of it."

~

Monkeys on meth. It was the only explanation. Broken glass crunched under Wheezy's sneakers. Every cabinet and drawer in the construction trailer hung open. The fridge door was torn off, contents splattered, tainting the air with raspberry vinaigrette.

"Christ," Wheezy said, ducking a red bra hanging from the ceiling fan.

He briefly considered the application of a flamethrower. But it was just a mess, handled like any other. The Z pattern applied.

For Wheezy it was more than method. It was prayer, poetry, and purpose – everything that allowed him to make sense of the world. The Z pattern had a rhythm, a flow, and a logical path. He'd pick a starting point and move side-to-side, corner-to-corner, and front-to-back. Sooner or later, order would be restored.

Wheezy snapped on blue gloves and shook open a trash bag. He got to work. Broken eggs were oozing through his fingers when the door swung open. Tammy stomped in, glittery-pink phone clamped to her ear, her face twisted into a scowl.

"Matter of fact, I do got one more thing to say, Carl. *Go fuck yourself!*" She slammed the phone shut and threw it across the room. The broken bottles in Wheezy's trash bag settled in a cascade of clanks. Tammy jumped. "Who the hell are you?"

Voice. Words. Speech. *Goddammit, say something.*

"Wheezy...I'm Wheezy. One of the custodians."

She pressed a tiny hand to her chest. "Baby, you scared me."

"Sorry." He stripped off his gloves and tossed them in the bag.

"That's okay," she said, waving him off. "You just wouldn't believe how many panty-sniffing creeps try to sneak in here."

She pulled the red bra from the fan blade and threw it at the mound of clothes on the couch. Her gaze travelled the length of the destroyed trailer. She turned back to him, cringing. "Dear Lord, what you must think of me."

Wheezy thought she looked older up close, mascara bleeding into the corrugations around her eyes, the skin over her forehead and cheekbones dry and tight. But her eyes retained their youthful clarity. Vivid aquamarine.

"Ain't right for you to clean up after me. I'll help." She picked up a sequined halter and folded it in thirds. A faded purple dragonfly on her back, wings worn thin, rippled with the motion of her arm. "Didn't I see you at the Winterbourne party tonight?"

"Doubt it," Wheezy said. "I was in the back."

"I always look in the back," she said, her dimple flickering on her cheek. "Didja like the show?"

The lie in his throat felt wrong, but the truth felt worse. He crouched to finish scraping up the eggs. *Say something.*

You're freaking her out. But he had no words. Tammy, his angel, was just a person. Flesh and blood. Breath and bone.

She grabbed the broom and avoided his eyes as she stabbed at the carpet with short strokes. Ceramic shards danced their way into a cluster. Wheezy was surprised she'd known that insider technique. He couldn't help smiling as he filled a bucket with hot water.

Tammy's broom rasped. Wheezy's sponge splatted. He wiped up the egg residue, and the salad dressing, then declared war on some stubborn mustard stains. When he finally looked up, he saw Tammy kneeling on the floor, tears curling down her cheeks like black ribbons.

"You okay?" he asked, sponge dripping on the carpet.

She glared at him through inky tears. "You think I like shakin' my ass for a living? Think I don't feel shit enough about it without you sittin' there, judging me?"

He dropped the sponge and knelt in front of her. "I'm sorry. I was just…surprised."

"I had a fight with Carl, my manager," she whispered. "He's sort of my boyfriend, too." She plucked an equine head out of the pile of shrapnel and sobbed. "He smashed my fucking unicorns."

Wheezy sat with Tammy on the sticky linoleum as she cried, cradling that unicorn head in her palm like a pearl. Finally, she held a wad of tissues to her nose and honked.

Wheezy was unexpectedly moved to run a washcloth under cold water and gently blot her streaky face. Her skin was warm and soft, like his dad's old undershirts. She smelled like soap and cigarettes. Mascara glued her eyelashes together in muddy clumps.

"Tammy, how is Carl sort of your boyfriend?"

She sniffed. "He loves me. But we don't, y'know, have S-E-X anymore."

"Oh."

"Gets what he needs from working girls."

"You're okay with that?"

"He takes care of me."

Wheezy blinked. "Let's clean up."

Two hours of side-to-side, corner-to-corner and front-to-back. The job was done. Wash water glugged down the sink drain. Tammy rifled through the cupboards and came up with nothing but a cereal bowl and a bottle of whiskey. She twisted off the cap and took a slug. Wiping her mouth with the back of her hand, her eyes revolved to meet his.

"Wouldja rather I drank it from the bowl?" she asked and offered him the bottle.

He shook his head.

They sat on opposite ends of the couch. Tammy kicked off her boots and tucked one tiny foot with purple lacquered toenails beneath her. She produced a pack of cigarettes and held it out to him. One a day was his usual rule, but sitting next to Tammy, he couldn't remember why.

"Hardcore," she teased when he tore off the filter and tossed it in the cereal bowl.

He felt his face redden. "I always smoke 'em this way."

She lit his and then her cigarette with a bedazzled pink lighter, noting his amusement. "Don't make faces," she said, blowing smoke out the corner of her mouth. "I like sparkles and I ain't ashamed to admit it."

"I wasn't—"

"So, tell me," she dabbed on some lip-gloss. "What the hell kind of name is Wheezy?"

He shrugged and exhaled.

Through the plume of smoke, he watched Tammy's eyes dart toward the door. She squirmed, her yellow skirt riding up on her thighs. She eyed the door again, got up and turned the lock.

"Tammy," he asked when she returned to the couch. "Are you in some kind of trouble?"

"Carl was looking for money." Trembling, she tapped her ash into the bowl. "But he's the one who takes care of that stuff. I'm lucky if I got a twenty in my purse."

She sloshed the whiskey around in the bottle. Wheezy thought maybe she was going to say something. She didn't. She took another pull from the bottle and again held it out to him. He tasted watermelon lip-gloss as the whiskey sizzled down his throat.

Tammy plucked at her bunched up skirt, exposing a large green bruise on her thigh. In a hushed monotone, she confessed that Carl liked to bet on the chucks – off track. He owed some scary people a whole lot of money, and they wanted it fast.

An icy millipede scurried between Wheezy's shoulder blades. Twenty-five years of criminal education had taught him a thing or two beyond the scope of the family business. No wonder Carl was sweating. When a shark called in your marker, you'd better make good.

"That's why I booked the Winterbourne show," Tammy said. "But I don't get paid until the end of Stampede, and it ain't enough, anyway. When I told Carl, he lost it. Wheezy, what am I gonna do?"

Wheezy lit another cigarette. On the way to Tammy's trailer, he'd sensed an imminent change in his life. He'd assumed for the better. "How much money are we talking?"

"We?"

"Tammy," he took her hand and her fingers laced through his. "How much?"

She took a last drag on her cigarette and crushed it out, moved the bowl to the end table and scooted onto the middle cushion, close to Wheezy. Her breath swirled hot in his ear and licked over his neck. She whispered a number.

The whispered figure was a lot. More than he'd expected. But it wasn't impossible. His stomach gurgled and burned. The Pepto-Bismol tablets were in his pocket but he didn't reach for them. Instead, he took another swig from the bottle.

It really was time.

~

Wheezy's scheme required prostitutes – lots of them. Unfortunately, he knew of only one person who could hook him up. Spencer's regular job was working custodial at a downtown nightclub where a lot of escorts arranged to meet their dates. The girls loved Spencer, not because he was polite, but because he was respectful. He was their baby.

"Wheezy." Spencer appeared around the corner of the Nashville North tent. "I talked to the girls. They'll help you if you can get them into the Winterbourne party on Saturday night."

Wheezy threw his pop can at the recycling bin. It swished through the round cut hole. Another cigarette clamped between his teeth, he dug his notebook from his pocket. Spencer arranged himself on the oil drum next to Wheezy's.

"You shouldn't smoke so much, Wheezy," Spencer said, pushing up his glasses.

Wheezy pulled another hand-rolled from his case, chain-lit it, and pitched the butt onto the asphalt.

Spencer extended his longer leg and crushed it out. "I'm not picking it up. You can do that."

Wheezy nodded. Then he did some math in his notebook. Good thing they were targeting two groups unlikely to have the first clue or care about street value. Made for easier gouging. Dragging deep on his cigarette, Wheezy handed Spencer a stack of envelopes. "For the girls."

Spencer tucked the invitations into his fanny pack.

Wheezy crushed out his third cigarette on the sole of his shoe and then bit into his ninth Pepto-Bismol. He was breaking every rule he had. He was dragging Spencer into a criminal enterprise. There was no right here. But Tammy needed help, she was in a mess and Wheezy was uniquely suited to clean it up. The Z pattern applied.

Besides, it was a one-off.

They're going to buy from someone, why not me? And I won't sell to anyone under sixteen, thought Wheezy. *Maybe fifteen.*

~

As planned, Spencer and his brigade of sex workers descended on the Winterbourne party while Wheezy hit up the teenagers clamoring for Random Hipster at the Coca-Cola stage.

Hidden in the mob, Wheezy schooled some kids on proper rolling technique. Past his audience, Spencer scampered toward him, fanny pack bobbing with every step.

"S'cuse me, folks," Wheezy said and passed off the neatly assembled joint.

"Do you have any more marijuana, Wheezy?" Spencer asked. "We're all out."

"Really? That's great." Wheezy shrugged off his backpack. He was running low on pot and his supply of Pepto and smokes had been decimated. But there was plenty of cash and that was what mattered. "Go ahead and take everything, Spencer."

A group of pimply boys was signaling him, so he left Spencer with the backpack while he went to make another deal. The boys were young, fourteen tops. But Wheezy had been smoking weed and tobacco since he was twelve years old, so what the hell?

Another rule broken.

By offering to roll, Wheezy managed to carve away an adolescent fortune for one damn joint. Spencer slid the strap of the backpack onto Wheezy's shoulder and scurried away, fanny-pack bulging.

In the last hour, Wheezy Barnes had burned through all his old rules and most of his new ones. His moral deregulation included corrupting Spencer, facilitating prostitution, and selling drugs to kids. But it was almost over. He would never do it again.

~

Nearly midnight, and Wheezy was waiting by the north gate for Spencer when two guys approached. They were about his age, clean-cut, scowling and tall.

"Hey," the tallest one said. "You Wheezy?"

He swallowed hard at a lick of nausea. "Sorry guys, all sales final."

"You've been working our turf," said the shorter one.

These guys are dealers?

Further thought on the matter was extinguished when pain bloomed on the side of his head and red petals unfurled down his neck. From there, it was a flurry of indistinct blows before he hit the pavement. A boot crunched against his ribs. He couldn't breathe. The world floated away…

"Wheezy. Wheezy, wake up."

The shaking jarred his ribs. "Unngh…stop…Spencer, stop. I'm awake. Just…gimme a fucking second," Wheezy groaned and wiped the blood out of his eyes.

Spencer stood back and started wringing his hands.

No flapping, Spencer. Please, no flapping. Wheezy gently touched his smashed face. His ribs were the worst, every breath loaded with ground glass, but nothing felt broken. The relief was short lived. Fifty feet away, on the pavement of the empty parking lot, was his ripped open backpack.

Oh, hell.

Wheezy pitched forward and vomited onto the asphalt. He was a bad person. What if those guys had rolled Spencer, or one of the girls? *This isn't me. I take care of people. I have rules. It's who I am.*

"Don't throw up, Wheezy." Spencer laid calm hands on Wheezy's heaving back. "We made enough money."

"Huh?" Wheezy wiped his mouth with his shirt.

"At the Coca-Cola stage. I did what you said. I took it all. The marijuana and the money. We have thirty-seven dollars extra."

A random volley of fireworks exploded in the sky. Wheezy smiled through the pain. "Spencer, you're the smartest person I know."

After what felt like the longest walk down the midway, Wheezy was once again standing outside Tammy's trailer. Raised voices punched through the steady rattle of the air conditioner.

"You lyin' little bitch! I want that money."

"You're coked out!"

A splintering crash.

Wheezy pulled the door open. A hollow-eyed man gripped Tammy's arm, his other hand cocked back in a fist. Carl.

"Git your hands off me!" Tammy twisted away, but not before Carl pinched her upper arm. "Ow!" she gasped. Her eyes popped wide, they were glassy. Had she been drinking? Wheezy thought he smelled whiskey.

"Beat it, kid," Carl said.

"Tammy?" Wheezy asked. "You okay?"

"You know this punk?" Carl's gaze ping-ponged between Tammy and Wheezy.

"Shut up, Carl," Tammy said, crossing her arms under her breasts. "Ain't no call to be rude. He's here to help."

"To help her." Wheezy hefted the backpack off his shoulder and handed it over to Tammy. "It's all there."

Carl laughed and wiped at his runny nose. "That's a whole lotta money, kid. I'm tellin' ya, this slut ain't worth it."

"Carl." She held out the backpack but kept her eyes on the floor. "You and me's quits. For good. Just take the money."

Carl snorted. "Got no use for a leathered-up gash like you, anyway." He snatched the bag from her hands, and tromped down the steps into the darkness.

Tammy stood at the open door, staring into the black. Her legs, exposed by a short, white robe, pebbled with goose bumps. Wheezy looked away, giving her time and space, just like he would with Spencer.

"He's a bad man," she said, quietly.

The night swallowed her words, just like it swallowed Carl.

"He's a bad man," she repeated, and then she shut the door. Delicate arches and sparkly toenails floated back and forth across the carpet.

"You okay?" Wheezy asked.

She glanced up, wearing a bashful smile that did things to him.

"Just realizin' that some dreams aren't meant to come true." She squeezed his hand and then dropped it. Her smile collapsed as she looked over his battered face.

"You're worth it," he said.

He took her hand. The front of her robe parted, exposing a wider expanse of skin. Again, he averted his gaze.

"It's okay to look," she said. "Everyone does."

"I don't want to look at you like everyone else."

"You ain't like everyone else, Wheezy. You ain't like *anyone* else." Her fingers caressed his split lip. "I just don't understand why you'd do something so incredible – so dangerous – for me."

"Because I love you," he blurted out.

Shit. Shit. Shit. The three words he'd promised he absolutely would not say.

"Why, Wheezy?" she whispered, eyes flooding with tears. "Why would you do that?"

Wheezy labored to swallow past the lump in his throat. She fell into his arms and he held her. It was all he could do. *Carl. Goddamn him.* But Carl was gone. And Wheezy knew this wasn't the time to play it safe.

"Tammy," he said, his lips brushing her hair. "For seven years, I thought I knew you. But then we met and you are so different. You smoke and drink and swear. But it's real, and it's better. It's only been a couple of days but…"

"Shh," she said and lifted her face up to his. "Y'know, my mama used to say it only takes one bitty moment to fall in love forever."

His heart drummed as her aquamarine gaze tore through everything that protected him. Her hands linked around his neck and for the first time in his life, Wheezy felt tall.

"I'm gonna kiss you, Wheezy."

He met her halfway, tasting watermelon and cigarettes, her lips soft and hot. His hands splayed over her back and her diamond-hard breasts crunched against his bruised ribs. She made a little *hmm* noise in her throat. And then it was over.

A girlish flush rose up her neck to her face. "Meet me at the west gate after the show tomorrow."

He stepped out of the trailer. But then he turned around. She was hugging the doorframe, one coltish leg crossed over the other.

"Tammy?" he asked, on a whim. "What's your real name?"

She looked down. That shy smile again. That dimple.

"It's Jane," she said with a lift of her shoulder. "Just Jane."

~

The next evening, a broom and some trash bags were all the ID he needed to get into the final Grandstand show. Tammy was introduced to a roaring wave of applause. She gave them what they wanted, some Faith, some Shania, some Patsy.

"Thanks y'all!" she shouted over the cheering. "Got one more song, one I never done before. Hope y'all like it."

The crew cleared the stage, leaving only a stool, a microphone, and an acoustic guitar. Tammy sat down, kicked off her silver heels and braced her dainty feet on the rungs of the stool. With bare fingertips, she began strumming. Then she started to sing a spare, acoustic version of 'The Bluest Eyes in Texas'.

A soft, husky voice, but strong enough to project even without a microphone. For the first time, in the glare of a single spotlight, accompanied by six strings, Tammy was singing as herself. As Jane.

Her eyes were closed. She played the chords and sang like a little girl with a big dream, sitting alone in her room, like no one was listening.

The moment was magic, but Wheezy was not spellbound. He knew what was real. His Tammy had been a paper doll. Jane was breath and bone. She sparkled. Her magic was real. What he felt was real.

The song ended to the distant rush of traffic. Then the crowd exploded. Tammy blew a single kiss to her fans and walked off the stage, guitar in hand. Her sparkling stilettos lay abandoned by the stool.

~

Midnight. Wheezy had all but worn a hole in his sneakers, pacing the uneven asphalt between the Round-up Center and the Coca-Cola stage. Maybe her phone was dead? Maybe she'd lost it? Why had she asked to meet here, anyway? Why not her trailer?

His feet skidded to a halt. His stomach twisted.

The duck hunting game on the midway was fixed. You could hit those pitted, tin quackers, again and again, and they wouldn't fall. Now, Wheezy saw inside the wheelhouse, and down came the ducks.

Carl, ready to punch her the exact moment Wheezy opened the door.

Carl, giving up just a little too quickly.

Tammy, of the black tears and shy smiles. A yellow skirt charming its way up a firm thigh. Smoky breath misting into his ear. A kiss flavored with watermelon and ashes.

He's a bad man.

Real bruises. Old ones. A cruel, unscripted pinch. Discarded silver shoes. Jane, singing with her eyes closed, in her own voice. A change of heart?

He's a bad man.

An air conditioner rattled in the distance.

Wheezy ran. And he ran.

~

Bridge

~

Spaghetti wilts in boiling water as I stir the marinara. Poured from a jar, not homemade. Pasta is the go-to these days. A culinary reflex. I'm beyond bored, but does it matter when everything tastes like nothing?

"Ev, can you tear up lettuce for a salad?" Sauce spatters on my blouse. Shit. I blot the red specks, knowing they've already established a covalent bond with the cotton fibers. I turn to my daughter. "Evelyn, I asked you to do something."

My seven-year-old sits at the table with her brushes and paint pots. Head down, arms curled around her paper. Painting, at least, is something. It's better than staring. Anything is better than that. The last few months have been hard on her. I just wish she'd talk to me.

"Ev?" I crouch by her chair and gently shake her shoulder. "Hey, moonwalker? Chow time on planet earth."

She looks up with that awful vacancy that makes me feel gauzy and insubstantial. Suddenly, she smiles and throws her arms around my neck. "Mama!"

There's no time to be stunned. I clutch her for as long as she'll allow. My eyes sting but I refuse to pollute this moment with tears. I've cried enough.

"I painted this for you, Mama."

She shoves the paper into my hand. The edge slices into the crease of my finger and blood weeps from the cut as I examine her work. Wet black paint covers every speck of white space in and around the subject: a bridge. The structure itself is brown, presumably made of wood. It curves over a black river, connecting two invisible banks. Crudely drawn, little more than smears of paint, and yet I find myself appreciating the Dali-esque curves, and the bold statement of a single object floating on a black canvas.

"My goodness," I murmur.

Evelyn nods. "I made it for you. Just for you."

"It's wonderful, Ev."

Wonderful. That's the word I use, though I'm quite sure it's not wonderful at all. Parents lie to their children all the time. For all sorts of reasons.

She pulls the picture from my hands and runs to the stairs. "I'm gonna hang it up."

"Okay, but then get your butt down here and make that salad."

She stampedes up the stairs, sounding for all the world, like a wildebeest. My daughter, the surrealist. Her walls are smothered in her creations already. I wonder where she'll find space for this one.

"Mama," she calls from the top of the stairs. "I'm outta tacks."

"Then steal one from another picture."

"Daddy has nails in his garage."

A shudder passes through me. By now, the spiders have almost certainly claimed the garage as their own. I've not been in there since Matt left. "Tacks only, Ev."

"Ugh. Okaaaay."

When I hear her bouncing around in her room, I slump against the wall. She's back. She's talking. There's too much inside me that wants out. I'll either scream and demand an explanation, or haul her into my arms and tattoo her with kisses until she simply won't have it. I bite down on my knuckles.

The pasta boils over.

After dinner, we manage a few minutes on Skype with Matt. His hair and lashes are chalky with the desert dust that keeps him elbow deep in seized up Humvees. Fortunately, all the grit in Afghanistan can't take the shine off his smile.

He seems a bit surprised when Evelyn jumps into frame, but listens attentively as she chatters on about the picture she painted just for me. When he asks what I've been up to, I tell him I rearranged the living room furniture according to Feng Shui. He laughs because it's bullshit. I laugh because he's laughing. And it is such bullshit.

"Change is good," he says. Then he tells me he'll be moving around for the next few days, and my buoyant mood sinks like a sack of hammers.

Moving around. On the road. I try not to think about it, but the acronym lights up the inside of my head. *IED*.

"Love you, babe. Give Ev a kiss for me. We'll talk soon, yeah?"

"I love you, too" *IED. IED. IED*. "Stay safe."

I close the Skype window and drop my face into my hands. Evelyn nudges her head under my arm. I kiss her shower damp earlobe, smelling tearless watermelon shampoo.

"Do you miss Daddy?"

I nod. "Yeah, I do. A lot."

She looks up at me, with her father's brown eyes. "Why don't you have a dream about him?"

"And how would I do that?"

"It's easy. Just think about Daddy when you're going to sleep. Think about him really hard, and he'll be there in your dream."

"Interesting theory." I stand up and take her hand. "Time for bed, Evvie."

~

Late evening creeps into middle night. I start a Dr. Phil book my mother gave me some years ago. I put down Dr. Phil. Think about calling my mother. I spill red wine on Dr. Phil. Maybe an accident. Maybe not, because I make no attempt to mop up the mess. The urge to call my mother passes. I trudge up the stairs toward the bed I haven't shared with my husband in almost four months.

I turn on my bedside light and slap my palm over my lips, muffling a startled squeak. Evelyn's painting hangs on the wall, a foot above my pillow. I move to take it down, but my fingers pause on the protruding nail. Did she sneak out to the garage? I don't want her out there.

The paint is still damp on the gently rippled paper. I don't like it at all, the aggressive arch of the bridge in a black void. But I care about it. I don't want to take it down. Evelyn made it for me.

While brushing my teeth, I notice the bathroom tap is dripping. A worn out washer. A broken seal. Easily ignored for the time being. I tug Matt's frayed Pearl Jam t-shirt over my head, the one that smells like motor oil no matter how many times I wash it. In bed, I hog the covers but remain on my half of the mattress. I'm nodding off when I remember Evelyn's hypothesis. Oh, what the hell. I plunge into the pool of recollection and see what I can dredge up.

Matt's hardened mechanic's hands braiding Evelyn's hair on picture day. Asymmetrical eyebrows that give him resting intrigue face. His catalogue of military grade profanity in reaction to stepping barefoot on Lego. The way he reaches for me in the dark, in his sleep, in this bed, pulling me close as though I'm a part of his body – something vestigial, given how easily he lives without me.

I bite into those memories and let their juices run down my throat. But I don't dream of my husband.

~

Leafy treetops flutter against the night sky and I hear the babble of moving water. I'm on a bicycle path, wearing only panties and Matt's shirt. I tug the hem down but it barely covers my ass. Does it matter? There's no one around, and it is a dream, after all. I should count myself lucky not to be naked.

A beckoning summer breeze whispers through my hair and I follow the asphalt around a curve, where the trees open up. On my left, the path drops sharply into a creek, the water sparkling like a vein of black diamonds. Perhaps fifty feet ahead, there's a bridge. I've seen it before. It's the wooden footbridge in the park not too far from our house. We've been riding our bikes here for years, though never after sundown.

Like Evelyn's painting, the scene is off somehow. Not quite right. My side of the forest glows silver under the stars. Across the creek, it's so dark I can't make out the demarcation between trees and sky. I plant my feet solidly on the path but the bridge tugs at my consciousness, yanking me from my own body like an arm from a sleeve. The bridge doesn't need my cooperation.

~

Tomato sauce heaves and erupts, splattering my blouse. Again. Damn it. Time to invest in an apron. The pasta boils over, hissing on the cooktop. Steam blurs my view of the table where Evelyn sits, painting.

"You're not tired of spaghetti?" I ask through the wet fog.

"Nope," she says.

"Why don't we do something different tomorrow? Chicken?"

Evelyn sweeps her brush over the soggy canvas. She's painting a picture, but it's not for me. That was last night. Or was it? I'm losing time. Used to be a few minutes here and there, but now it seems an entire twenty-four hour chunk can flit past without any meaningful memory. Does it matter when each day is the same as the one before?

Later, Matt's pixilated image appears on the computer, desert winds blowing behind him. We chat for a few moments as a family and then I leave to allow him a moment alone with Evelyn. When she comes out of the den, it's my turn.

"Moving on pretty soon," he says. "Might not be in touch for a while."

"You said that yesterday."

He frowns. "Did I?"

"Something's wrong with Evelyn."

"She's worried about you, too. Says she painted you a picture. She thought it would help."

My hands grow clammy. "I'm in a funk, I guess. Can't seem to snap out of it."

"People snap all the time." The lines on his face betray a deeper sadness than I have words for. "Kim, I know you don't want to hear this, but I need you to really listen..."

His lips move, but the sound cuts out. Then the video. He's gone. He's going on the road. Those last words could've been *the* last words. He was telling me something I needed to know. And I lost him.

I go upstairs and find Evelyn sitting up in her bed with the lamp on, staring blankly at the wall covered in her artwork.

"Hey, Ev. What are you doing up?"

She blinks and turns her head toward my voice. "You forgot to tuck me in."

I sit on the edge of her bed and she scoots into my lap. She's been waiting for me this whole time. I forgot about her. It's almost midnight. I couldn't have been talking to Matt that long. What was I doing then? Sitting in the dark?

"I'm sorry, Ev. I'm so sorry."

Evelyn pulls away and cups my face in her hands. "Mama, I don't want you to be sad anymore."

She's the one who looks sad. The lamplight forms a pink halo around her, but there are murky smudges under her eyes. Even at supper she looked pale and drawn.

"You feeling okay, baby?"

She frowns, looking just like her father. "I'm tired."

We both are. We're in a rut. When was the last time we got out? I kiss the top of her head. "What do you say we go for a bike ride tomorrow?"

"Bikes are in the garage, Mama."

"Yeah, I know..." my voice turns to powder in my throat, which I cover with a cough. "I know where they are."

She lies down and I tuck the covers in around her. With her face pressed against my hip, she falls into deep sleep. I stay for a long time. When she was a newborn, I'd sit by her crib for hours, unable to tear myself away. Matt humored me, but I knew he was relieved when I stopped the endless sleep watching. Years later, I'm doing it again, but it's different. Her sleep is different. I'm different. Not. Quite. Right.

Later, in my own room, with my face washed, teeth brushed, wearing Matt's old shirt, I study the painting above my pillow. When I trace the curve of the bridge with my finger, it makes an unpleasant dusty sound, like whispered secrets you never wanted to know.

I should take it down. I want to. I can't.

~

163

Another moonless night, maybe the same night. My bare feet straddle the middle line of the path as I follow the creek upstream. Stars light my way, but across the water there is only black. The bridge looms ahead. Last time it turned me inside out. This time I don't resist the pull. The deck is coarse and splintered under my feet, the rail is winter cold in the warm night, and I'm not alone.

At the other end of the bridge, there's a girl, I think, in a white nightie. I can't see her face but I hear her breathing, a dry scrape, over the gentle splash of the creek below. Step-by-step, we meet in the middle. Her matted hair swarms over the black pits of her eyes and her arms are little more than bones with peeling grey skin stretched over them. I think of scarecrows.

"Who are you?" I ask.

The creature's shoulders heave as she fills lungs that sound like paper bags full of sand. Behind her, on the dark side of the bridge, the forest seems to move. Thick shadows weave together to conceal whatever stirs there. Nothing that hides in that kind of darkness can be good. The creature's pallid lips move. She's trying to tell me something, but the only sound is that dusty rasp.

"I don't understand."

She shuffles closer. I see mottled scalp where clumps of hair have fallen out. She lunges and I leap back, just beyond the reach of her skeletal claw. She bares her teeth in a grimace while muddy tears pour from her eye sockets down her sunken cheeks.

"I'm sorry," I whisper. "I can't help you. I have to go home."

I turn and race back the way I came. My feet thud over the wooden planks and then slap on asphalt. I follow the path into the starlit safety of the forest. I run until my feet bleed.

~

Coffee. God of morning. Patron saint of the sleep-deprived. Bitter and blistering hot in the World's Best Dad mug Evelyn gave Matt last Father's Day. I blow on the surface, stirring up a gentle wake. A sigh from the stairs distracts me from my ritual.

"Ev?" I look up and nearly drop my mug. "Evvie?"

She's halfway down the stairs, clinging to the rail. Aside from the dark mass of bed hair and the purple circles under her eyes, she's completely colorless. Bleached.

"Mom," she says and her knees buckle.

Coffee sloshes, burning my hand as I slide the mug onto the counter and rush up the steps. I expect her body to be cooking with fever, but she's cold. She's too big for carrying but I hoist her up anyway and carry her to my bed. She sinks into my pillow and her bruised eyes open, glazed.

"Can we watch cartoons?"

I find SpongeBob on the television. Then I crawl into bed with her, holding her until she passes out in deep, cold sleep.

My plan is to get up and call the doctor, but I'm already drifting into a dreamless twilight. Only the steady drip of the bathroom tap anchors me to consciousness. I can fix it, but I'd have to get the wrench from the garage.

~

When I open my eyes, it's dark out. An entire day gone, but at least I didn't dream. Evelyn stirs. I wince as a flurry of pins and needles attacks the arm that's been trapped under her.

"It's nighttime," she croaks, backlit by the muted television. "Can we talk to Daddy?"

I shake the sensation back into my arm. "Daddy can't talk right now...he's on the road."

"Gonna check the computer. Just in case he left a message," she says and scuttles off the bed, showing a little more energy than she had in the morning. It won't last long. This isn't right. I need to get her to the doctor, maybe even the children's hospital.

But I don't.

I follow her downstairs, sparing a backward glance for the painting above my bed. A bridge over black water.

"See? I told you," says Evelyn, when I open my laptop.

An invite for video chat blinks on the screen and Matt's grinning face fills the window. "How're my ladies?"

I leave Evelyn to chat privately with her daddy. It's important for them to have that time.

"She's sick," I say to him, after Evelyn says her goodbyes and goes back upstairs to lie down. "I told you there's something wrong with her."

"You look tired," he says.

"Don't change the subject."

"You can't keep this up. None of us can."

"I thought you were on the road."

"Just because the lights are on, doesn't mean anyone's home."

"Matt, you're scaring me."

"For Christ's sake, why won't you listen?"

Listen to what? I feel like we're having two different conversations. Why can't he just say what he means? Unless he's not at liberty. Classified information.

He shakes his head. "Babe, I can't help you from here. I tried...but it's up to you."

I'm completely out of it from sleeping all day and I don't know what he wants. Even if I did, I'm not sure I could give it to him. The last time we spoke face-to-face was in the garage. We had a terrible argument.

"Are you angry with me?" I ask.

He looks down for a long moment. "Not anymore."

I wipe my eyes with the front of the Pearl Jam t-shirt. "I'm sorry. I just wish we could be together."

"So do I." He kisses his fingertips and presses them to the screen. "I love you, Kimmy. But my time is up."

The house collapses into darkness when I close my laptop. Upstairs, I find Evelyn in my bed, asleep again. I'm dead tired myself and I feel the dream in the wings of my consciousness, anxiously waiting to take the stage. In the bathroom, I open the medicine cabinet and take out my prescription bottle of Ambien. Sixty nights worth of dreamless blotto. When I pop the cap, however, it's empty. I know I took some when Matt first left and I wasn't used to sleeping alone. Only a few though, at least I thought it was just a few. Missing pills. Missing time. My eyelids roll down like heavy overhead doors. Time's up. I stumble into bed and curl around my sleeping daughter. I don't want to dream. I don't have a choice.

~

Across the water, the forest is dark and fibrous as ever. I'm on the path but I don't see the bridge. A leaf floats down and sticks to my cheek. It came from the sky, smells like the earth, and clings to me, an object in between. I peel the leaf off my face and let it blow away.

The bridge appears, blending with the landscape, showing itself when and to whom it chooses. There's a reason I'm here. A connection I'm missing.

I step onto the deck and find the little wraith right where I left her, huddled in the center of the bridge, hugging her knees – a brokenhearted cry lurching out of her body. The thought of touching her shrivels the skin between my shoulder blades, but monstrous as she is, she's still a child. I'm still a mother.

I step toward the center of the bridge. "Sweetheart, are you all right?"

She doesn't react at all. It's like she can't hear me, like I'm not here, and suddenly I want more than anything for her to acknowledge me. To look up, to smile, to come alive, and show me…show me a picture.

An icy breath shivers through my lips. "Evelyn?"

She lifts her head and the black portals of her eyes meet mine. "Mama."

I rush to the middle of the bridge, fall on my knees, and pull her into my arms. And it *is* her. Emaciated, eyeless. But under the smell of dust and decay, it's tempura paint, watermelon shampoo, and a thousand other notes comprising an olfactory signature I'd know anywhere.

Another sob ripples through her body. "Mama, I'm tired."

Of course she's tired. She's trapped in a rotting corpse. It must be exhausting. How did my daughter die?

"Evvie, what happened?"

"I can't wait anymore," she wails and clings to me.

It's not a child's impatience. She's telling me this is our last chance. One way or another, I will never see this bridge again.

"We shouldn't be here." I try pulling her with me towards the light side of the bridge, but she won't budge. "Ev, we need go home."

"Daddy said you wouldn't listen."

"What?"

"Nobody's home, Mama."

I step away from my child and in the starlight I see the grey tatters of skin hanging off my own arms. I press my hands to my face. The bones of my fingers sink into empty holes where my eyes should be. This whole time I've been blind.

~

Matt looks up from the gutted Chevy when I throw the garage door open so hard it bangs against the wall. He's wearing old jeans and an even older Pearl Jam t-shirt. Soon, he'll be in fatigues. Again.

"You promised this wouldn't happen."

He sighs. "I didn't think it would."

"Last time a bomb went off right under you. For days, I didn't know if you were alive or dead. No one could tell me anything. I can't do that again, Matt. I can't."

He sets the socket wrench down on the workbench and gathers my hands into his, smearing grease over my knuckles. "Babe, I'm sorry, but they need all the mechanics they can get. It's the dust. Gets into everything."

"You should have been killed," I whisper. "Everyone says so."

"I know, I got lucky."

"No one is that lucky. If you go back there…I'm just being mathematical."

"Or hysterical," he mutters, dropping my hands, grabbing a pair of pliers and diving back under the hood of that fucking truck that will never leave our fucking garage because he'll never stay home long enough to finish the fucking thing. "I need you to get right with this, Kim. It can't be like last time. I can't be over there, worried that you're losing your goddamn mind here."

I slam my fist down on the workbench. My jaw quivers with rage. "Don't you dare treat me like some unhinged harridan when I'm stuck here raising our daughter alone, not knowing if you'll come back. You think that's easy?"

He glances up. "Compared to living in a war zone? Yeah, I do."

He falls, knocking over a bucket of spent motor oil that pools around him in striking contrast to the blood spilling from his head. Red and black swirl together like Evelyn's paints. Only a few missing seconds. But there he is, skull punched in, eyes empty. And here I am, fingers wrapped around the socket wrench, knuckles jutting like teeth under my skin, under my husband's greasy fingerprints.

People snap all the time.

That night, I bring Evelyn into my bed and we burrow together under the blankets. Her, in a white nightgown. Me, in a freshly laundered Pearl Jam t-shirt that still reeks of motor oil. She finished her hot chocolate, though she said it tasted funny, and the World's Best Dad mug sits on the nightstand next to my empty water glass. We're a family, I remind myself, and all I want – all I've ever wanted – is for us to be together.

Evelyn emits a squeaky yawn. "Where's Daddy?"

The pillow beneath my cheek discreetly absorbs my tears, and I'm thinking of a place, somewhere antithetical to the desert that pulled him away from us so many times.

"Ev, do you remember the bridge in the park? The one with all the trees where we ride our bikes?"

"And throw rocks in the creek?"

I nod. "That's where Daddy is, and we're going to meet him there."

"But…it's nighttime…I'm tired."

"I know, baby. We're going to sleep, and when we wake up, we'll be on the bridge. You might get there first, but I'll be right behind you, so I want you to wait for me, okay? Promise?"

She nods against my heavy heart. I give her a squeeze and I don't let go until my arms are too heavy, and then numb, to hold her.

~

On the bridge, Evelyn's gritty breath rattles in my ears and her fingers dig into my shoulders. "I waited, Mama. Right here, like you said. But you didn't come."

I wasn't ready. Too many regrets. I wanted to wake up and start over. So I did. Over, and over, and over. But the dust gets into everything, and it slowly clogged the hidden gears of my delusion. Now, here we are. Mother and daughter, a pair of grotesques, not meant for any heaven. Does it matter, when I've already spent god knows how long in hell?

Evelyn's dead hand grips mine. "Come on, Mama. Come with me."

I follow my daughter across the bridge, into the darkness, where Matt is waiting and we will be a family again.

~

Suicide Stitch

~

I stood on my sister Celia's clover infested lawn as the dumpster slid off the truck and settled on the driveway with a steely boom. I'd ordered the biggest, knowing I'd need it emptied at least once before I was done. The driver lowered the hydraulic bed. I gave him a thumbs-up and he drove off in a rumbling diesel crescendo.

The edges of Celia's key dug into my palm as I turned back to the house with its scabby brown paint and leaky windows. Once I got the front door open, I had to kick a trail through a heap of garment bags just to get past the gloomy foyer. I reached for the light switch but let my hand drop short. Full exposure could wait.

I peered into the living room, finding it crammed full of boxes and bags containing buttons, zippers, snaps, rivets, thread, and piping. A mountain of notions so high it brushed the beards of dust hanging from the motionless ceiling fan. I shoved my way through more garment bags and slipped down the hall, sideways, on account of the bolts of fabric stacked up against the walls on either side. I knew it would be bad. When it comes to hoarders, there is no rock bottom, not until you've hit the rafters.

"Damn it, Celia," I muttered. I'd been doing that a lot the last few days. Damning her. For being a complete fuck up. For leaving me with this disaster. For ripping a vital stitch out of my life without any warning. I wasn't ready to sort through her shit and clean up her mess. I wasn't ready for my little sister to be dead.

My phone burbled in my skirt pocket. I scanned the screen. My thumb hovered over the decline button. Except I knew he'd only keep calling. I brought the phone to my ear. "Hey, Nate."

"Hi." He paused and I heard a whining roar in the background, which meant he was driving. "I've been trying to call you for days. Min, I'm so sorry."

"Thanks."

Why did I thank him? Why did he apologize? He didn't do anything, and I wasn't grateful. That was the problem with us; our deferent lies came automatically. Truth had always been a weapon of last resort.

"It was a car accident?" he asked.

"That's what the constable said."

"But you told them."

"Told them what?"

"Your sister wasn't exactly stable, Min."

"Doesn't matter anymore." Layers of puddled fabric baffled my voice into a flat slurch of sound. More lies. Of course it mattered. If it really were just an accident, I probably wouldn't be here.

"Are you all right?" Nate asked, engine revving. "Do you need help?"

"Celia's the one who needed help." I wandered into the kitchen and headed toward the stairs. "And the whole point of divorce is for you to extricate yourself from my life, not weave your way back into it. At least that's the impression you gave me when you asked for one."

"C'mon, Min. Don't be like that…"

He might have trailed off. More likely, I stopped listening. Because I saw her. Above me, on a steel pedestal in the middle of the landing that split the steep staircase into two manageable halves. Buff canvas stretched over a woman-shaped torso. She faced me head on – much as a headless woman can – her curves pleasing, her posture inscrutable. Sunshine poured through the window behind her, and her shadow yawned down the stairs towards me.

"Min?"

"Gotta go."

"Wait—"

"I found Dolly," I said and hung up, shoving the phone in the pocket of my skirt. Celia knew I liked pockets and always found a way to sew them into my skirts and dresses.

From my vantage point, Dolly looked as big as she had the day my grandma brought her home for Celia and I when we were nine and ten years old, respectively. Grandma was a seamstress and she planned to teach us her trade. My first turn at her old Kenmore sewing machine, I stomped on the peddle before lowering the pressorfoot. Grandma had to yank the needle out of my fingertip with pliers. From there, she decided it might be best to teach us to sew by hand. But my stitches were uneven, my seams crooked, and the fabric consistently ended up dotted with specks of blood.

Celia though…

In her little hand, the needle became a magic wand. Within a week, she'd turned out a whole dress. Nothing fancy. Just a blue shift, but her seams were strong and straight. Her stitches, meticulous.

"I'm going to kill myself."

"Huh?" I looked up from my math homework.

"Not today.

"Tomorrow?"

"Probably not for a long time," she said, sitting down across the table, resting her chin in her hands. "I have to make a perfect dress first."

"That one you just made is perfect. Grandma said."

"Dolly says the zipper is uneven. Just a little."

"Who's Dolly?"

"The dress form."

"Dress forms don't have names."

"She says that once you've done something perfect, there's no point doing anything else."

"You're a weirdo."

Celia bounded over to my side of the table and grabbed me up in a hard hug. I wasn't expecting it and my pencil lead pricked my neck.

"Don't worry, Min," Celia said. "I promise not to kill myself without saying goodbye first."

And so it went through our teens, twenties, and thirties. Periodically, I'd get a voicemail, email, or once, a registered letter, saying something like, 'Thursday', or 'Sunday', or whatever. A terse missive indicating the date she expected to finish her magnum opus. I'd go to her house on that day, and I'd have to find the tiny flaw in an otherwise perfect dress. A tailor made game of Where's Waldo. I figured she was sloppy on purpose, on account of her not really wanting to kill herself but being too proud to renege on an oath she took as a nine-year-old. Don't get me wrong: the dresses were works of art with an inner light and life of their own. She sold them on the Internet, complete with the one small Waldo that she always left uncorrected.

"Say this dress was the one," I posited, after identifying a poorly executed blanket stitch on a buttonhole. "How would you do it?"

She gave me a despondent shrug and unzipped the yellow frock. The bodice slipped down Dolly's molded breasts and dropped into the skirt pooling at the pedestal base. "Swallow a bunch of pills, maybe...or pins. Y'know, whatever's around. Ought to be spontaneous, don't you think?"

Then her eyes, the deep slate of black pearls, welled up. She gathered the yellow dress in her arms, hugging it for a moment before tossing it on her worktable and shuffling over to me. I tucked her head under my chin and held her as she cried out her obvious frustration and secret relief.

I hiked up to the landing and rested my hands on Dolly's shoulders. "Didn't expect you to be naked."

Truly I didn't. Why wasn't she in the sewing room, haloed by the sun, wearing a diaphanous, petal pink gown? I always imagined that perfect dress being pink. No idea why.

I curled an arm around Dolly's waist and hauled her up the next flight of steps, trying not to trip on the grocery sacks stuffed with brown tissue paper patterns and piles of remnants in an endless array of colors.

How Celia found anything in this nut house, I could never figure out, but she had a system. I could ask her for the teal zipper from a tartan skirt she wore when she was sixteen and she'd buzz down to the basement, make a hell of a lot of noise, and minutes later, be back in her sewing room, teal zipper in hand.

A fat tear licked down my cheek. I wiped it away and cleared a passage to the sewing room. The door swung open without meeting any obstructions. I carried Dolly inside and set her down on the dust-free floorboards. The sewing room was the one orderly space in the house. And militantly so. Afternoon light came in through a clean window over a large, uncluttered worktable. I sat down at the smaller sewing table that held Grandma's heavy old Kenmore. I rested my forehead on the cold enamel, smelling machine oil and synthetic fibers. Then I got up and opened the closet.

Several dresses hung from the rod. Red strapless tea length. Blue maxi dress. Slinky plum wrap. A chartreuse number with a tutu skirt that should have been hideous but was, instead, strangely adorable. All lovely, but none perfect. I'd post them on eBay as usual.

"Well, Dolly?" I glanced over at the dress form. "Care to point me in the right direction?"

Dolly stood, impassive.

"Fine, but I know it's here somewhere, and I'm going to find it." I got up and strode out of the room, flicking Dolly's left breast as I went by.

The front door seemed a logical starting point. I opened each sticky plastic garment bag clogging the foyer and sorted through their rumpled contents. Mostly thrift shop rags destined for repurposing. No dresses. I dragged the bags and clothes by the armful out to the driveway where I tossed them over the lip of the bin.

Next, I tackled the hallway. The purge would move faster if I could at least get from the front of the house to the back without turning sideways. I carried bolts of fabric, three at a time, out to the bin. Wool, linen, poly blend, satin, crepe, and a variety of knits. In they went. Deep jewel tones, delicate pastels, and smart geometric patterns. My sister's shattered rainbow of accumulation thudded to the bottom of the dumpster.

My phone buzzed in my skirt. I checked the screen. An email. From my lawyer. Not my divorce lawyer, my traffic court lawyer. Reminding me of my appearance next Tuesday. I'd already paid the fine and had the Breathalyzer system installed, but I needed to shave some demerits off my license before my insurance came up for renewal.

The whole thing was mortifying. I'd been upset on account of a fresh firing from the tool rental place – or was it the caterer's? Sometimes my resumé blurred into a single grey streak of failure. Anyway, I'd lipped off an obnoxious customer. Can I help it if I have a medical condition? My manager humorlessly informed me that a 'severe asshole allergy' wasn't a thing and tossed me out on my ear. I bounced my way to the nearest bar. A series of poor choices followed.

Darkness fell, forcing me to turn on a few lights. I finished clearing the hallway sometime near midnight, my hands and arms raw with fabric burn. Tomorrow, I'd wear long sleeves and a pair of work gloves. I slid down cool plaster to the floor, and stretched my legs out across the newly exposed hall runner – vibrant cobalt, a faded stripe worn down the center from years of Celia's sidling down the narrow passage she'd left between bales of textiles.

I blotted the sweat behind my ears with a scrap of cotton. Burnt orange paisley. I'd bought it myself envisioning a simple sundress. A few days later, Celia had whipped up a sheath cut on the bias with a fringed hemline. You know, the opposite of what I'd asked for.

On Dolly the sheath looked fabulous. On me it looked like a lampshade. Until Celia attacked with a mouthful of pins and commenced pinching, tucking and gathering. A vein pulsed blue on her pale forehead. The color of concentration. Of course, the dress wasn't perfect. The hem dropped slightly in the back, a flaw easily interpreted as a deliberate stroke of style. Even her mistakes were meticulous.

Sprawled in the hot, dim hallway, I hiked my skirt up and draped the paisley over my bare legs. So cool and soft. Nate never understood Celia, but he loved that dress. I tipped my head back recalling how his hand strayed to my lap under the restaurant table, wedding band grazing my thigh as he worried the silky bronze fringe between his fingers.

That was before. And now?

Nate. Gone.

Celia. Gone.

Me. Alone. With a Breathalyzer in my car and all my seams coming apart.

I dragged myself off the floor and walked down the hall, arms out, fingers brushing the walls on either side. I wanted to go home and have a drink. Vodka, with a splash of lime, or some other dilutive technicality. Instead, I locked the front door, switched off the lights and made my way upstairs, gathering up an endless bridal train of tulle as I went. In the sewing room, silvered by moonlight, Dolly stood on her pedestal, facing the door. Had I left her that way? I dumped the bundle of tulle in the corner and approached.

"Sorry about earlier." I gently twisted the dials on her chest, waist, and hips. *Click, click, click.* "Guess I'm a little jealous. She never talked to me the way she talked to you."

I closed Dolly right up to a size zero, approximating Celia's petite dimensions. The waist still wasn't small enough. My sister wore steel-boned corsets that, over the course of two decades, had irreparably mutilated her rib cage. She never denied being self-destructive; she just didn't think it was a problem.

"Celia, you can't live on alphabet soup."

"But I like it."

"It's not about what you like," I said, holding a can of Campbell's in each hand. "Wearing a torture device that forces you onto a liquid diet is not healthy."

Celia cocked her hip, emphasizing the brutally cinched middle under her polka dot shirtwaist. "If anyone drinks too much, Minnie, it's you."

I tightened my grip on the soup cans. "Do you have any idea what I'm going through right now? Nate moved out, work is bad, I'm not sleeping, and now I'm worried about you not eating."

"I know, Minnie, I know, I know..." Her hands reached up to cool my cheeks. I leaned into her and dropped my head on her shoulder. I let my delicate doll of a sister hold me up and stroke my hair. "You worry too much. Why can't you believe that I'm happy? Just because you don't understand the way I live."

That was the worst part. I *did* understand. I just couldn't accept. Saving Celia from Celia had been my purpose since I could remember. Since Grandma died, I'd sacrificed a career, friends, and probably my marriage to make sure my sister showered at least once a week, turned off her stove, and paid her utility bills. I put the sprinkler on her grass in the summer, turned her furnace on in the winter, and kept her hoarding in check all year round. Most importantly, I found those clever mistakes in her work. But what if Celia didn't need saving? A person who truly intended to kill herself would not be dissuaded, no matter how many shoddy blanket stiches I pointed out.

Dolly's minimized form detached easily from the pedestal and I carried her into Celia's bedroom where the quilt was thrown back in a jumble, the depression of her body still outlined on the bottom sheet. I shed my clothes and crawled into the twin bed, pulling Dolly in with me under the covers. I turned my nose into the pillow. The sheets were dirty, saturated with the smell of Celia's hair and sweat. A good smell on account of the fact that even at age thirty-five, Celia perspired like a child. Honey and salt, grimy and golden, like the food you buy at a fairground.

I hugged Dolly's unyielding flesh, wetting her canvas skin with my tears. I imagined her phantom arms holding me the way I'd held Celia after every failed attempt at perfection, each slender stay of execution. She promised she wouldn't leave. Not without saying goodbye. The only promise she'd ever made, to my knowledge. I drifted off knowing that, somehow, I had failed her.

A gale rattled the windowpanes and shrieked under the eaves of Grandma's house. I rolled on my side, facing the wall, even as I heard a whimper, the rustle of blankets, and the slap-slap-slap of bare feet. Nine-year-old Celia clambered into my bed and squirmed up against my back. I felt the chill of her through my jammies. Cold-blooded, she was, like a reptile, warming only to the temperature of her immediate environment.

A spray of lightning threw Dolly's eerily stretched silhouette against the wall. Thunder cracked like a whip.

Celia shoved her face between my shoulder blades. "Min, I'm scared."

"It's just a storm."

"Can I sleep with you?"

I huffed into the crook of my arm. "You're too old to be crawling into my bed every time it rains."

"Dolly says you can protect me."

I looked over my shoulder at the dress form standing by the closet. I hated her. Hated that she shared our room. Shadow rivulets of rain trickled down her body. Then her dials began to turn. Click, click, click. I went rigid as her seams opened wider and wider, until the stuff inside, the black blood that made her Dolly, rather than just a dress form, poured out in sheets.

Lightning flashed. Thunder blasted.

"Minnie!" Celia wailed.

"It's okay, it's okay." I wound my arms around her quaking little body. "Don't be scared. I'll keep you safe."

I woke up shivering in a bright pool of sunlight from the east-facing window. "Oh…fuck," I groaned, my head full of mud and my mouth dry as talc. The worst hangover in history and I'd consumed not a drop of alcohol. Bad dreams will do that to you. Which probably explained why I drank so much in the first place.

"Dolly?" I flipped through the covers, searching for my best frenemy, as if she were as easily lost in the sheets as an iPhone – which just then buzzed from the pile of clothes I'd left on the floor. I hand-walked off the bed far enough to grab the phone out of my skirt pocket and then retreated back under the covers.

"Hey," I croaked.

"Did I wake you?" Nate asked.

"Yeah," I replied, thinking I might as well let him feel bad about it. "Got kinda late last night so I stayed over."

Nate's nose-breathing shushed into the phone. "You sure that's such a good idea?"

"Jesus…" I pulled the pillow over my head. "The only contact we've had in weeks has been through our lawyers, and now you're concerned with what's good for me?"

"Why don't I come over, bring coffee, some food, maybe? Help you clear out all that garbage."

A part of me – a large lonely part – wanted to say yes, wanted to fill the hole in my heart with something, anything, even Nate. But rage got there first. "Garbage? Where do you get off calling her life garbage?"

"Minnie…"

His misguided use of the sisterly appellation sealed his doom. I leapt out of bed and paced back and forth between the closet and window. Righteously indignant in my panties. "You left me, Nate. Because you didn't want to share. Now you think that because I don't have to look after her anymore, you can stampede back into my life and everything'll be perfect?"

"I left because you wouldn't listen to reason," he snapped. "I couldn't watch you get dragged down with her. So, if Celia's death gives you a chance to really live for the first time, then yeah, maybe I don't think that's the worst thing in the world."

"Go to hell, you son of a bitch." I cranked the window open, punched out the screen, and chucked the phone into the clear blue sky. A second later, I heard it pong against the dumpster below. Not hell, but close enough.

I stomped into the bathroom and turned on the shower. Hot water slowly rumbled through the old pipes. Gave me time to think. Nate hadn't deserved that, but I wasn't exactly sorry for saying it. I needed to assign fault and unleash my emotional hurricane on someone. Nate saw Celia as the root of all my problems. Which made him sort of stupid. He sneered at my devotion to the only family I had. Which made him sort of mean.

The mirror fogged over. I pulled back the shower curtain and stepped into the grungy tub, finding half a bar of ivory soap and a lime scaled razor in the dish. Objects in situ. After my shower, I wrapped myself with a cleanish towel and used Celia's toothbrush. I didn't relish the idea of slipping back into my sweaty clothes from yesterday, but none of Celia's tween-sized get ups would fit.

I stepped out of the bathroom and into a long shadow reaching out of the sewing room door. My heart clobbered my sternum and I tightened the musty towel around my chest. The shadow shifted slightly.

"Celia?"

My voice burned off my lips like morning fog. I didn't expect a reply from my dead sister, but was nevertheless disappointed by the answering silence. I took three steps forward and pushed the sewing room door wide open.

"Oh," I said. "There you are."

Dolly. Back on her pedestal, and this time she wasn't naked. I supposed I could have done it. Sleepwalking or some such. Or someone could have broken in, pulled Dolly from my sleep-dead arms, and dressed her up. Hell, as long as I was flinging ridiculous hypotheticals, Dolly might have managed it, herself, with her no-arms. I ought to have been scared. Except the 'how' of it didn't seem to matter as much as the 'why'.

A breeze from the open window feathered my damp hair. I was wrong. The dress wasn't pink. And of all the colors in the kaleidoscope Celia worked in, I'd never once known her to eschew color altogether. But there it was.

A full-skirted gown of black silk, draped and swirled in dramatic arcs. Shivering in the draft like an obsidian butterfly. No weapon could have looked more lethal.

The plunging neckline exposed the reopened seam bisecting Dolly's chest. I didn't have to see her dials to know the measurements. 35-27-37. I dropped my towel. Lots of women wore a size six but this was no coincidence.

Carefully, I lifted the gown off Dolly and dropped it over my head. Cool silk whispered against my skin. Unlike the spotty bathroom mirror, the full-length glass in the sewing room gleamed pristine silver. I pulled up the side zipper and studied the dress from every angle. A flawless fit. The dress that murdered my sister was made for me. Its living curves transformed me into the cruel beauty I'd always been on the inside.

I slid my hand through folds of midnight and into the pocket I knew I'd find there. Something pricked my finger. I pulled out a gold needle stuck through a spool of black thread. She'd left it in the pocket. For me. I stared at that spool for a long time, until I could no longer avoid the obvious conclusion.

Celia's accident was really just an accident. She didn't break her promise. Somewhere on this black beauty, I would find something left undone or poorly finished. I fell to my knees, skirt billowing around me. I pulled the hemline through my fingers inch-by-inch, examining each fine stitch, until I found it – a pinkie's width of raw edge.

No one was perfect. But this dress could be. I could finish what my brilliantly insane little sister had come so close to accomplishing. Celia wanted this. She needed it.

Actually, Celia doesn't need anything. On account of her being dead. Remember? You ID'd her body. She's dead. Your sister is dead...

No matter how many times I slapped myself with the words, they never penetrated. My brain couldn't unravel me from her. Couldn't stitch together a reality in which I was alive and my sister was not. All these years, I'd tried to save her.

I gazed up at the dress form with her cracked open seams. She was the one who'd understood, and I'd held her in such contempt. I reached up and stroked her hard hip.

"Thank you, Dolly."

Then, I licked the end of the thread, slid it through the eye of the needle, and with more precision than I'd applied to anything else in my life, I finished the hem. Double knot on the last stitch, just like Grandma taught us. I lifted the scissors off their designated hook above the worktable. Pulled the dangling thread tight.

Snip.

I twirled slowly in front of the mirror, admiring how the sunlight died a shimmering death on contact with black silk. I twirled once more. Then I placed the still-threaded needle on the back of my tongue and swallowed.

~

Acknowledgments

~

This collection stands on too many shoulders to count. Teachers, tush kickers, editors with a taste for the weird, and people who didn't sign up for this but got on board anyway. Rea Tarvydas, who challenged me to write my first short story (Wheezy thanks you). My crit partner Robin van Eck, who made the mistake of leaving my cage open. Gaurav Sethi, blog brother and Van to my Ada. My parents, who let me read everything. Jerry, my marvelous Spousal Unit, and a man brave enough to share his bed with someone who writes this stuff. Auntie Donna, who read my early work and with a straight face told me to keep at it. And my editor, Jen Word, who stitched this creature together and fed it commas until it could walk on its own. Honestly, I could fill a book with all the people I want to thank. I hope you know who you are and how grateful I am.

About the Author

~

Sarah L. Johnson lives in Calgary where she runs marathons, blogs about Nabokov, and occasionally overuses the word perpendicular. Her short fiction has appeared in Room Magazine, Shock Totem, and the Bram Stoker nominated Dark Visions 1. Her first novel *Infractus* is coming soon from Driven Press.

Check out www.sarahljohnson.com for more information and inconsistent blogging.

~

54067289R00114

Made in the USA
Charleston, SC
25 March 2016